THE DEMONATA

SLAWTER

✦ ✦ ✦

BY DARREN SHAN

Ⓛ Ⓑ   AUG   2016

LITTLE, BROWN AND COMPANY
New York Boston

For:
first assistant director: Bas "lurhmann"
hair by: "Figaro" Brian
screenwriting muse: Lynda "minder" Lewis
spliced together by: Stella "stargate" Paskins
a Christopher Little studios production

Little, Brown and Company

Hachette Book Group
237 Park Avenue, New York, NY 10017
Visit our website at www.lb-teens.com

Little, Brown and Company is a division of Hachette Book Group, Inc.
The Little, Brown name and logo are trademarks of Hachette Book Group, Inc.

The publisher is not responsible for websites (or their content) that are not owned by the publisher.

First U.S. Hardcover Edition: November 2006
First U.S. Paperback Edition: November 2007
First published in Great Britain by Collins in 2006

The characters and events portrayed in this book are fictitious.
Any similarity to real persons, living or dead, is coincidental
and not intended by the author.

Library of Congress Cataloging-in-Publication Data
Shan, Darren.
  Slawter / Darren Shan. — 1st U.S. ed.
    p. cm. — (The Demonata ; bk. 3)
  Summary: While on a horror movie set with his Uncle Dervish, Grubbs Grady realizes that his battle with the evil demon master Lord Loss may be about to resume.
  ISBN 978-0-316-01387-1 (hc) / ISBN 978-0-316-01388-8 (pb)
  [1. Demonology — Fiction. 2. Magic — Fiction. 3. Motion pictures — Fiction. 4. Horror stories.] I. Title. II. Series: Shan, Darren. Demonata ; bk. 3.
PZ7.S52823Sla   2006
[Fic] — dc22   2005030800

10 9 8 7 6 5 4 3

RRD-C

Printed in the United States of America

PART ONE

✠ ✠ ✠

VISITORS

LIFE AS WE KNOW IT

✛   ✛   ✛

My eyes! They stabbed out my eyes!"

I shoot awake. Start to struggle up from my bed. An arm hits the side of my head. Knocks me down. A man screams, "My eyes! Who took my eyes?"

"Dervish!" I roar, rolling off the bed, landing beside the feet of my frantic uncle. "It's only a dream! Wake up!"

"My eyes!" Dervish yells again. I can see his face now, illuminated by a three-quarters-full moon. Eyes wide open, but seeing nothing. Fear scribbled into every line of his features. He lifts his right foot. Brings it down towards my head — hard. I make like a turtle and just barely avoid having my nose smashed.

"*You* took them!" he hisses, sensing my presence, fear turning to hate. He bends and grabs my throat. His fingers tighten. Dervish is thin, doesn't look like much, but his appearance is deceptive. He could crush my throat, easy.

I swipe at his hand, yanking my neck away at the same time. Break free. Scrabble backwards. Halted by the bed.

Dervish lunges after me. I kick at his head, both feet. No time to worry about hurting him. Connect firmly. Drive him back. He grunts, shakes his head, loses focus.

"Dervish!" I shout. "It's me, Grubbs! Wake up! It's only a nightmare! You have to stop before you —"

"The master," Dervish cuts in, fear filling his face again. He's staring at the ceiling — rather, that's where his eyes are fixed. "Lord Loss." He starts to cry. "Don't . . . please . . . not again. My eyes. Leave them alone. Please . . ."

"Dervish," I say, softly this time, rising, rubbing the side of my head where he hit me, approaching him cautiously. "Dervish. Derv the perv — where's your nerve?" Knowing from past nights that rhymes draw his attention. "Derv on the floor — where's the door? Derv without eyes — what's the surprise?"

He blinks. His head lowers a fraction. Sight returns gradually. His pupils were black holes. Now they look quasi-normal.

"It's OK," I tell him, moving closer, wary in case the nightmare suddenly fires up again. "You're home. With me. Lord Loss can't get you here. Your eyes are fine. It was just a nightmare."

"Grubbs?" Dervish wheezes.

"Yes, boss."

"That's really you? You're not an illusion? *He* hasn't created an image of you, to torment me?"

"Don't be stupid. Not even Michelangelo could sculpt a face this perfect."

Dervish smiles. The last of the nightmare passes. He sits on the floor and looks at me through watery globes. "How you doing, big guy?"

"Coolio."

"Did I hurt you?" he asks quietly.

"You couldn't if you tried," I smirk, not telling him about the hit to the head, the hand on my throat, the foot at my face.

I sit beside him. Drape an arm around his shoulders. He hugs me tight. Murmurs, "It was so real. I thought I was back there. I . . ."

And then he weeps, sobbing like a child. And I hold him, talking softly as the moon descends, telling him it's OK, he's home, he's safe — he's no longer in the universe of demons.

✠ Never trust fairy tales. Any story that ends with "They all lived happily ever after" is a crock. There are no happy endings. No endings, full stop. Life goes on. There's always something new around the corner. You can overcome major obstacles, face great danger, look evil in the eye, and live to tell the tale — but that's not the end. Life sweeps you forward, swings you around, bruises and batters you, drops some new drama or tragedy in your lap, never lets go until you get to the one true end — death. As long as you're breathing, your story's still going.

If the rules of fairy-tales *did* work, my story would have ended on a high four months ago. That's when Dervish regained his senses and everything seemed set to return to normal. But that was a false ending. A misleading happy pause.

I had to write a short biography for an English assignment recently. A snappy, zappy summing-up of my life. I had to discard my first effort — it was too close to the bone, and would only have led to trouble if I'd handed it in. I wrote an edited, watered-down version and submitted that instead. (I got a B minus.) But I kept the original. It's hidden under a pile of clothes in my wardrobe. I dig it out now to read, to pass some time. I've read through it a lot these past few weeks, usually early in the morning, after an interrupted night, when I can't sleep.

I was born Grubitsch Grady. One sister, Gretelda. Grubbs and Gret for short. Normal, boring lives for a long time. Then Gret turned into a werewolf.

There's a genetic flaw in my family. Lots of my ancestors have turned into werewolves. It hits in your teens, if you're one of the unlucky ones. You lose your mind. Your body alters. You become a blood-crazed beast. And spend the rest of your life locked up in a cage — unless your relatives kill you. There's no cure. Except one. But that can be even worse than the curse.

See, demons are real. Gross, misshapen, magical beings, with a hatred of humans matched only by their taste for human flesh. They live in their own universe, but some can cross into our world.

One of the Demonata — that's the proper term — is called Lord Loss. A real charmer. No nose or heart — a hole in his chest full of snakes. Eight arms. Horrible pale red flesh. Loads of cuts on his body, from which blood flows in a never-ending stream. He's big on misery. Feeds off the unhappiness, terror, and grief of humans. Moves among us silently when he crosses into our universe, invisible to normal eyes, dropping in on funerals the way you or I would pop into a café, dining on our despair, savoring our sorrow.

Lord Loss is a powerful demon master. Most masters can't cross from their universe to ours, but he's an exception. He has the power to cure lycanthropy. He can lift the curse from infected Grady teenagers, rid them of their werewolf genes, return them to humanity. Except, y'know, he's a demon, so why the hell should he?

"What are you reading?"

It's Dervish, standing in the doorway of my room, mug of coffee in one hand, eyes still wide and freaky from his nightmare.

"My biography," I tell him.

He frowns. "What?"

"I'm going to publish my memoirs. I'm thinking of *Life with Demons* as a title. Or maybe *Hairy Boys and Girls of the Grady Clan*. What do you think?"

Dervish stares at me uneasily. "You're weird," he mutters, then trudges away.

"Wonder where I get that from?" I retort, then shake my head and return to the biography.

Luckily for us, Lord Loss is a chess addict. Chess is the one thing he enjoys almost as much as a weeping human. But he doesn't get to play very often. None of his demonic buddies know the rules, and humans aren't inclined to test their skills against him.

One of my more cunning ancestors was Bartholomew Garadex, a magician. (Not a guy who pulls rabbits out of a hat — a full-fledged, Merlin- and Gandalf-class master of magic.) He figured out a way to cash in on Lord Loss's love of chess. He challenged the demon master to a series of games. For every match Bartholomew won, Lord Loss would cure a member of the family. If old Bart lost, Lord Loss would get to torture and kill him.

Bartholomew won all their matches, but future members of the family — those with a flair for magic, who made contact with Lord Loss — weren't so fortunate. Some triumphed, but most lost. The rules altered over the years. Now, a parent who wants to challenge Lord Loss needs a partner. The pair face not only the master, but two of his familiars as well. One plays chess with the big guy, while the other battles his servants. If either loses, both are slaughtered, along with the affected teen. If they win, one travels to Lord Loss's realm and fights him there. The other returns home with the cured kid.

Time works differently in the universe of the Demonata. A year of our time can be a day there, a decade, or a century. When the partner goes off with Lord Loss to do battle, their body remains in our world — only their soul crosses over. They become a mindless zombie. And they stay that way unless their soul triumphs. If that happens, their mind returns and they resume their normal life. If they don't fare so well, they stay a zombie until the day they die.

"Are you coming down for breakfast?" Dervish yells from the bottom of the giant staircase that links the floors of the mansion where we live.

"In a minute," I yell back. "I've just come to the part when you zombied out on me."

"Stop messing around!" he roars. "I'm scrambling eggs, and if you're not down in sixty seconds, too bad!"

Damn. He knows all my weaknesses.

"Coming!" I shout, getting up and reaching for my clothes, tossing the bio aside for later.

✠ Dervish does a mean scrambled egg. Best I've ever tasted. I finish off a plateful without stopping for breath, then eagerly go for seconds. I'm built on the big side — a mammoth compared to most of my schoolmates — with an appetite to match.

Dervish is wearing a pair of sweatpants and a T-shirt. No shoes or socks. His grey hair is frizzed, except on top, where he's bald as a billiard ball. Hasn't shaved (he used to have a beard, but got rid of it recently). Doesn't smell good — sweaty and stale. He's this way most days. Has been ever since he came back.

"You eating that or not?" I ask. He looks over blankly from where he's standing, close to the stove. He's been staring out the window at the grey autumn sky, not touching his food.

"Huh?" he says.

"Breakfast is the most important meal of the day."

He looks down at his plate. Smiles weakly. Sticks his fork into the eggs, stirs them, then gazes out of the window again. "I remember the nightmare," he says. "They cut my eyes out. They were circling me, tormenting me, using my empty sockets as —"

"Hey," I stop him, "I'm a kid. I shouldn't be hearing this. You'll scar me for life with stories like that."

Dervish grins, warmth in it this time. "Take more than a scary story to scar you," he grunts, then starts to eat. I help myself to thirds, then return to the biography, not needing the sheet of paper to finish, able to recall it perfectly.

I have a younger half-brother, Bill-E Spleen. He doesn't know we're brothers. Thinks Dervish is his father. I met him when I came to live with Dervish, after my parents died trying to save Gret. (I spent a while in a loony asylum first.)

Bill-E and I became friends. I thought he was an oddball, but harmless. Then he changed into a werewolf. Dervish explained the situation to me, told me Bill-E was my brother, laid out the family history and our link to Lord Loss.

I wasn't eager to get involved, but Dervish thought I had what it takes to kick demon ass. I told him he was nuts but . . . hell, I don't want to come across all heroic . . . but Bill-E was my brother. Mom and Dad put their lives on the line for Gret. I figured I owed Bill-E the same sort of commitment.

So we faced Lord Loss and his familiars, Artery and Vein, a vicious, bloodthirsty pair. I got the better of Lord Loss at chess, more by luck than plan. The demon master was furious, but rules are rules. So I got to return to reality along with the cured Bill-E. And Dervish won himself a ticket to Demonata hell, to go toe-to-toe with the big double L on his home turf.

I'm not sure what happened there, how they fought, what sort of a mess Dervish went through, how time passed for him, the manner of his victory over Lord Loss. For more than a year I guarded his body, helped by a team of lawyers (my uncle — he mucho reeeech) and Meera Flame, one of Dervish's best friends. I went back to school, rebuilt my life, and babysat Dervish.

Then, without warning, he returned. I woke up one morning and the zombie was gone. He was his old self, talking, laughing, brain intact. We celebrated for days, us,

Bill-E, and Meera. And we all lived happily ever after. The end.

Except, of course, it wasn't. Life isn't a fairy tale. Stories don't end. Before she left, Meera took me aside and warned me to be careful. She said there was no way to predict Dervish's state of mind. According to the recorded accounts of the few who'd gone through the same ordeal as him, it often took a person a long time to settle after a one-on-one encounter with Lord Loss. Sometimes they never properly recovered.

"We don't know what's going on inside his head," she whispered. "He looks fine, but that could change. Watch him, Grubbs. Be prepared for mood swings. Try and help. Do what you can. But don't be afraid to call me for help."

I did call when the nightmares started, when Dervish first attacked me in his sleep—mistook me for a demon and tried to cut my heart out. (Luckily, in his delirium, he picked up a spoon instead of a knife.) But there was nothing Meera could do, other than cast a few calming spells and recommend he visit a psychiatrist. Dervish rejected that idea, but she threatened to take me away from him if he didn't. So he went to see one, a guy who knew about demons, whom Dervish could be honest with. After the second session, the psychiatrist called Meera and said he never wanted to see Dervish again — he found their sessions too upsetting.

Meera discussed the possibility of having Dervish committed, or hiring bodyguards to look after him, but I rejected both suggestions. So, against her wishes, we carried on living by ourselves in this spooky old mansion. It hasn't been too bad. Dervish rarely gets the nightmares more than two or three times a week. I've gotten used to them. Waking up in the middle of the night to screams is no worse than being disturbed by a baby's cries. Really it isn't.

And he's not that much of a threat. We keep the knives locked away, and have bolted the other weapons in the mansion — it's filled with axes, maces, spears, swords, all sorts of cool stuff — to the walls. I usually keep my door locked too, to be safe. The only reason it was open last night was that Dervish had thrown a fit both nights before, and it's rare for him to fall prey to the nightmares three times in a row. I thought I was safe. That's why I didn't bother with the lock. It was my fault, not Dervish's.

"I will kill him for you, master," Dervish says softly.

I lower my fork. "What?"

He turns, blank-faced, looking like he did when his soul was fighting Lord Loss. My heart rate quickens. Then he grins.

"Ass!" I snap. Dervish has a sick sense of humor.

I get back to wolfing down my breakfast, and Dervish tucks into his, not caring that the scrambled eggs are cold. We're an odd couple, a big lump of a teenager like me playing nursemaid to a balding, mentally disturbed adult like Dervish. And yeah, there are nights when he really frightens me, when I feel like I can't take it anymore, when I cry. It's not fair. Dervish fought the good fight and won. That should have been the end of it. Happy ever after.

But stories don't end. They continue as long as you're alive. You just have to get on with things. Turn the page, start a new chapter, find out what's in store for you next, and keep your fingers crossed that it's not *too* awful. Even if you know in your heart and soul that it most probably will be.

PRAY AT HIM

✠ ✠ ✠

School was strange when I first went back. I'd spent months outside the system, first in the asylum, then in the mansion with Dervish. It took me a while to find my feet. For the first couple of terms I didn't really speak to anybody except Bill-E and the school guidance counselor, Mr. Mauch, better known as Misery Mauch because of his long face. I'd always been popular at my old school, lots of friends, active in several sports teams, Mr. Cool.

All that changed at Carcery Vale. I was shy, unsure of myself, reluctant to get involved in conversations or commit to after-school events. On top of the hell I'd been through, there was Dervish to consider. He needed me at home. I became an anonymous kid, one who spent a lot of time by himself or with a similarly awkward friend (step forward Bill-E Spleen).

Things are different now. I've come out of my shell a bit. I'm more like the old me, not quiet in class or afraid to speak to other kids. I've always been bigger than most people my age. In the old days I was a show-off and used my bulk to command respect. At the Vale I kept my head bent, shoulders hunched, trying to suck my frame in to make myself seem smaller.

Not anymore. I'm no longer Mr. Flash, but I'm not hiding now. I don't feel that I have to.

I've made new friends. Charlie Rall, Robbie McCarthy, Mary Hayes. And Loch Gossel. Loch's big, not as massive as me, but closer to my size than anybody else. He wrestles a lot — real wrestling, not the showbiz stuff you see on TV. He's been trying to get me to join his team since I started school. I resisted for a long time, but now I'm thinking of giving it a go.

Loch also has a younger sister, Reni. She's pretty cute, even if she does have a nose that would put Gonzo to shame! I stare at her a lot of the time, and sometimes she makes eyes back. I think she'd go out with me if I asked. I haven't. Not yet. But soon . . . maybe . . . if I can work up the nerve.

✠ The end of a typical school day. Yawning through classes, desperate for lunchtime, so I can hang out with my friends and chat about movies, music, TV, computer games, whatever. Bill-E joined us for some of it. I don't spend as much time with Bill-E as I used to. He doesn't fit in with my new friends — they think he's geeky. They don't mouth off about him when I'm around, but I know they do when I'm not. I feel bad about that, and try to help Bill-E relax, so they can see his real side. But he gets nervous around the others, acts differently, becomes the butt of their jokes.

Thinking about Bill-E as I walk home. I don't want us to stop being friends. He's my brother, and he was really good to me when I first moved here. But it's difficult, because I don't want to lose my new friends either. Guess I'll just have to work harder to make him feel like part of the group. Try and be like one of those TV kids who always solve their problems by the end of each show.

Dervish is sitting on the stairs when I let myself in. I'm dripping wet — it's been pouring for the last couple of hours. Normally, when the weather's bad, he picks me up on his motorcycle. When there was no sign of him today, I figured his mood hadn't improved since breakfast. I was right. He's as blank as he was this morning, staring off into space, not registering me until I'm right in front of him.

"Dervish! Hey, Derveeshio! Earth to Dervish! Are you reading me, captain?"

He blinks, frowns as if he doesn't know who I am, then smiles. "Grubbs. You're alive. I thought . . ." His expression clears. "Sorry. I was miles away."

I sit beside him. "Bad day?"

"Can't remember," he replies. "Why are you home early?" I hold up my watch and tap it. Dervish reads the time and sighs. "I'm losing it, Grubbs."

My insides tighten, but I don't let Dervish see my fear. "Losing what — your sanity? You can't lose what you never had."

"My grip." Dervish looks down at his feet, bare and dirty. "I wasn't like this before. I wasn't this distracted and empty. Was I?" He looks at me pleadingly.

"You've been through hell, Derv," I tell him quietly. "You can't expect to recover without a few hiccups."

"I know. But I wasn't this way, right? Some days I can't remember. I feel like it's always been like this."

"No," I say firmly. "It's just a phase. It'll pass."

"All things must pass," Dervish mutters. Then he looks at me sideways, his cool blue eyes coming into focus. "Why are you wet?"

"Took a bath. Forgot to strip." I rap his forehead with my knuckles, then point to the windows and the rain battering the panes. "Numbskull."

"Oh," Dervish says. "I should have picked you up."

"No problem." I rise and stretch, dripping steadily. "I'm going up to shower and change into dry clothes. I'll stick these in the wash. Anything you want me to add?" I did all the jobs around the house when Dervish was a vegetable. Hard to break the habit.

"No, I don't think so. I . . ." Dervish stares at his left hand. There's a black mark on it, a small "d." "There was something I meant to tell you. What . . . ?" He snaps his fingers. "I had a phone call, a follow-up to some e-mails I've been getting recently. Ever heard of a someone called Davida Haym?"

"No, can't say . . ." I pause. "Hold on. Not David A. Haym, the movie producer?"

"That's her."

"I thought that was a guy."

"Nope. She uses David A. on her movies, but it's Davida. You know about her?"

"Sure. She makes horror movies. *Zombie Zest. Witches Weird. Night Mayors* — that's, like, *Nightmares*, only two words. It's about evil mayors who band together to set up a meat production plant, except the meat they process is human flesh."

"Win many Oscars?" Dervish asks.

"Clean sweep," I chuckle. "I can't believe she's a woman. I always thought . . . But what about her? I didn't think you were into horror flicks."

"She called me earlier."

I do a double-take. "David A. Haym called you?"

"Davida Haym. Yes." Dervish squints at me. "Have I grown a second head?"

"Hell, it's David A. Haym, Dervish! That's like saying Steven Spielberg was on the line, or George Lucas. OK, not as big as those, but still . . ."

"I didn't know she was famous," Dervish says. "She told me the names of some of her movies, but I don't watch a lot of films. She made it sound like she was a cult director."

"She is. She doesn't make films with big-name stars. But her movies are great! Anyone who loves horror knows about David A. Haym. Though I'm not sure many know she's a woman."

"That's a big sticking point for you, isn't it?" Dervish grins. "You're not turning into a chauvinist, are you?"

"No, I just . . ." I shake my head. Water flies from my ginger hair and splatters the wall. "What did she want?"

"She's making a new movie. Asked if she could meet me. She'd heard I know a lot about the occult. Wants to pick my brain." He tweaks his chin, forgetting the beard isn't there. "I hope she didn't mean that literally."

"Did you say yes?" I ask, excited.

"Said I'd think about it."

"Dervish! You've got to! It's David A. Haym! Did she say she'd come here? Can I meet her? Do you think —"

"Easy, tiger," Dervish laughs. "We didn't discuss where we'd meet. But you think I should agree to it?"

"Absolutely!"

"Then meet we shall," Dervish says, getting to his feet and heading up to his office. "Anything to please master Grady."

I tramp up the stairs after him, pulling off my clothes, thinking about how cool it would be if I could meet David A. Haym . . . and also how weird it is that one of the world's premier horror producers is a woman.

✠ "David A. Haym's a woman? No bloody way!" Loch howls.

"You're putting us on!" Robbie challenges me.

"How stupid do you think we are?" Charlie huffs.

"Of course she's a woman," Mary says. We gape at her. "You didn't know?"

"No," Loch says. "You did?"

"Yes."

"How long?"

Mary shrugs. "I dunno. Years."

"And you never told us?" Robbie barks.

"It never came up," Mary laughs. "I have no interest in horror movies. I always tune out when you guys start on that garbage."

"Then how did you know she's a woman?" I ask.

"There was a feature on her in a magazine my mum reads," Mary explains. "I think the headline was, 'The horror producer chick who beats the boys at their own game.'"

They're nearly as excited as I am. Most of my friends don't

know what to make of Dervish. In a way he's cool, the adult who rides a motorcycle, dresses in denim, lets me do pretty much what I like. On the other hand, he sometimes comes across as a complete nutcase. Plus they know he was a vegetable for more than a year.

But now that he's in talks with the slickest, sickest producer of recent horror movies, his cred rises like a helium balloon. They want to know how she knows about him, when she's coming, what the new movie's about. I act mysterious and secretive, giving nothing away, but dropping hints that I'm fully clued-in. In truth, I know no more than they do. Dervish wasn't able to get through to her last night. He left a message and was waiting for her to call back when I left this morning.

✠ "Did she call?"

"Who?"

I groan, wishing Dervish wasn't a complete airhead. "David A. Haym, of course! Did she —"

"Oh, yeah, she called."

"*And?*" I practically shriek, as Dervish focuses on getting dinner ready.

"She'll drop by within the next week."

"Here?" I gasp. "Carcery Vale?"

"No," he smirks. "*Here* — this house. I told her she could stay the night if she wanted, though I don't know if —"

"David A. Haym's going to stay in our house?" I shout.

"Davida," Dervish corrects me.

"Dervish . . . the terrible things I've said about you . . . the awful names I've called you . . . I take them all back!"

"Thanks," Dervish laughs. Stops and frowns. "*What* awful names?"

✠ Everyone wants David A. Haym's autograph. They want to meet her, have dinner with us, maybe snag a part in her next movie. Loch auditions for me several times a day, moaning and screaming, pretending bits of his body have been chopped off, quoting lines from *Zombie Zest* and *Night Mayors* — "We elected a devil!" "That's not *my* hand on your knee!" "Mustard or mayo with your brains?" Draws curious stares from teachers and kids who haven't heard the big news.

Bill-E tosses around script ideas. Figures he can pitch to her and become the brains behind her next five movies. "Writers are getting younger all the time," he insists. "Producers want fresh talent, original ideas, guys who can think outside the box."

"You're about as far outside the box as they come," Loch laughs.

"I wouldn't have to write the whole script myself," Bill-E says, ignoring the jibe. "I could collaborate. I'm a team player."

"Yeah," Loch snorts. "Trouble is, you're a substitute!"

I let them scheme and dream. Smile smugly, as if they're just crazy, dreamy kids. Of course, I'm as full of wild notions as they are — I just prefer to play it cool.

✠ Days pass — no sign of Davida Haym. The weekend comes and goes. I bug Dervish constantly, asking if there's been any further contact. Sometimes he pretends he doesn't know what I'm talking about, just to wind me up.

By Tuesday I'm starting to wonder if it's a gag, if Dervish never spoke to David A. Haym at all. It would be a weird, unfunny joke — but Dervish is into weird and unfunny. I'll look like an idiot in school if she never shows. I'll have to invent a story, pretend she was called away on an emergency.

Thinking about excuses I could use as I'm walking home. Nothing too simple, like a sick relative or having to pick up an award. Needs to be more dramatic. Her house burned to the ground? She caught bubonic plague and had to go into isolation?

Warming to the plague theory — can people get it these days? — when a car pulls up beside me. A window rolls down. A thin, black-haired woman leans across. "Excuse me," she says. "Do you know where Dervish Grady lives?"

"Yeah." I bend down, excitement building. "I'm his nephew, Grubitsch. I mean, Grubbs. Grubbs Grady. That's me." Can't remember the last time I called myself Grubitsch. What a dork!

"Grubbs," the woman says, nodding shortly. "Yes. I know about you."

"You do?" Unable to hide my delight. "Dervish told you about me? Wow, that's great! Uh, I mean, yeah, cool. I know about you too, of course."

"Really?" She sounds surprised.

"Sure. I've been waiting all week for you."

"You knew I was coming?" Sharp this time.

"Yeah. Dervish told me."

She taps the steering wheel with her fingernails. They're cut short, down to the flesh. "Well, may I give you a lift home, Grubbs? That way you can direct me as we go."

"Sure!" I open the door and slide in. Put my seat belt on. Smile wide at David A. — I mean, Davida — Haym. She smiles back thinly. A narrow, pale face. Moody, if not downright gloomy. Exactly the way I expected a horror producer to look. "Just go straight," I tell her. "The road runs by our house. You can't miss it — only mansion in the neighborhood."

Silence. Davida is focused on the road. I'm trying to think of something to say that's casual and witty. But my mind's a blank. So I check her out. Thin all over, a long neck, bony hands, straight black hair, dark eyes. Dull white shirt and skirt. Flat, plain shoes. No jewelry, except one ring on her left hand with a large gold "L" in the middle of a circle of flat silver.

"How have you been, Grubbs?" she asks suddenly.

"Fine."

"I know something of your past. What happened last year with Billy Spleen."

"What do you know about me and Bill-E?" I ask suspiciously, guard rising.

"I know about the lycanthropy. How you fought it."

"Dervish told you *that*?" I cry, astonished.

"How has Billy been? Any recurrences of his old patterns?"

"Of course not! We cured him! He's normal now!"

"And you?" she says quietly, and her eyes flick across, cold and calculating.

"Who the hell are you?" I ask, a tremble in my voice.

"Who do you think I am?" she replies.

"I thought you were David A. Haym. But you're not . . . are you?"

In answer she raises a finger and points. "That must be the mansion."

She pulls into our drive. I have a bad feeling in my gut, not sure who this woman is or how she knows about Bill-E. The woman kills the engine and looks at me calmly. Her eyes are *really* dark. A robot-like expression. No makeup. Thin lips, almost invisible. A small nose with a wartish mole on the right nostril.

"Shall we go in together, or do you want to go ahead and tell your uncle that I'm here?" she asks.

"That depends. What's your name?" She only smiles in reply. She looks more normal when she smiles, like a teacher — stern, but human. I relax slightly. "You can come with me," I decide, not wanting to leave her here in case she's an old friend of Dervish's and I appear rude.

"Thank you," she says and gets out of the car. She's smoothing her skirt down and studying the mansion when I step out. "Nice place," she comments, then raises a thin eyebrow, the signal for me to lead the way. I start ahead of her, whistling, not letting her see that I'm unnerved, acting like she's an ordinary visitor. In through the oversized front doors. The juicy smell of sizzling steak drifts from the kitchen.

"Goodness," the woman says, looking at the high ceiling, the size of the rooms, the weapons on the walls, the staircase.

"This way," I tell her, heading for the kitchen. "You're just in time for dinner."

She follows slowly, absorbing the surroundings. Obviously

hasn't been here before. I keep trying to put a name to her face, thinking of all the people Dervish has mentioned in the past.

I reach the kitchen. Dervish is hard at work on the steak. "No!" he shouts before I say anything. "She hasn't called and there's been no sign of her. Now stop pestering me, or I might —"

"We have company," I interrupt.

Dervish turns questioningly. The woman enters the kitchen. I step aside so he can see her. Instant recognition. His face goes white, then red. He steps away from the stove, abandoning the steak. Eyes tight. Lips quivering. With anger.

"*You!*" He spits the word out.

"It's been a long time, Dervish," the woman says softly, not moving forward to shake his hand. "You look better than I expected."

"I thought she was David A. Haym," I tell him.

"She's not," he barks. "She's Prae Athim."

"Pray at him?" I echo.

"Pray Ah-teem," the woman says, stressing the syllables.

"She's one of the Lambs," Dervish says with a sneer.

And the fear that was tickling away at me in the car kicks in solid, like a nail being hammered into my gut.

LAMBIKINS

✣   ✣   ✣

IN Dervish's study. Like most of the rooms, it's huge. But whereas the others have bare walls, with stone or wood floorboards, the study is carpeted and the walls are covered with leather panels. There are two large desks, bookcases galore, a PC, laptop, typewriter, paper, and pens. There used to be five chess sets, but not anymore. The swords and axes that hung from the walls are gone too.

Prae Athim doesn't want me here. That's obvious from her disapproving look. Dervish doesn't care. He's seated behind the computer desk, one hand on his mouse, moving it around in small circles, waiting for his unwelcome guest to speak. Prae Athim is seated opposite. I'm standing close to the door, ready to leave if Dervish tells me to.

"Billy Spleen still lives with his grandparents?" Prae says finally. Dervish nods slowly. "I thought you might have moved him in with you. To observe."

"You're the master observer, not me," Dervish says quietly.

"Isn't it dangerous, leaving him there?" she presses.

"Billy's time of turning has passed. There's nothing to fear from him now."

"That's debatable," Prae smiles.

"No. It isn't."

Prae looks at her hands, crossed over her lap. Thinks a moment. Then nods at me. "I'd rather not speak in front of the boy."

"Is this about him?" Dervish responds.

"Partially."

"Then you'll have to."

"I really don't think —" she begins.

"Grubbs faced the demons with me," Dervish interrupts. "He fought by my side. I'm not going to keep secrets from him."

"Really?" Prae sniffs. "You tell him everything about your business?"

"No. But I don't hide things from him. When he asks, I answer. And since I'm certain he's going to be asking about this, he might as well stay and hear it firsthand."

Prae sighs. "You never make life easy for us. You've always treated the Lambs like enemies. We're on the same side, Dervish. You should give us respect."

"I do respect you," Dervish says. "I just don't trust you."

I'd forgotten about the Lambs. They loomed large in my thoughts while Dervish was zombified, especially around the time of a full moon. If I'd found myself turning into a werewolf, I was going to phone them and ask them to put me out of my misery. But since Dervish returned, I haven't had time to brood about my potentially fatal genes, or the family bogeymen.

The Gradys and their kin have been cursed for a long time. We're talking a *lot* of generations. Over the centuries, family members have tried to figure out the cause of the curse, find a cure for it, and develop ways of dealing with the infected children quietly and efficiently.

The Lambs are the result. A group of scientists, soldiers, and I don't know what else, all focused on the problems and logistics of lycanthropy. They spend a lot of time, money, and effort trying to unlock the secrets of the rogue Grady genes. But they also play the part of executioners when necessary.

A lot of parents decide to kill their children if they turn into werewolves. But most can't perform the dirty deed themselves. So they call in the Lambs, who take the transformed child away and do what must be done.

"How did you find out about Billy?" Dervish asks.

"We keep tabs on all the family children," Prae says.

"But Billy didn't leave a trail. There was no evidence that he was turning."

Prae smiles. "You covered up admirably. Gathered the bodies of the animals he slaughtered, disposed of them quietly. But you couldn't be expected to find *every* corpse. And you couldn't do anything about the operative who saw him sneaking out of his house during a full moon."

"You had him under direct surveillance?" Dervish snaps.

"Sometimes, yes."

Dervish's hand goes rigid on the mouse. "You had no right to do that."

"We had every right," Prae disagrees. "If a guardian chooses to deal personally with an infected child, it's not our business. But you didn't. You gave him free rein."

"I was in control," Dervish growls. "He wasn't a danger to anyone. I was waiting for the right moment to act."

"I understand," Prae says. "But we couldn't take any chances. We guessed you would handle the matter this way if he turned, so for some years we'd been keeping an eye on the boy. On your brother's children too."

Dervish starts to retort. Stops and scowls. "Tell me why you've come."

"A few reasons," Prae says. "One — to make sure Billy is normal."

"He is," Dervish says. "We cured him."

"But how certain is your 'cure'?" Prae asks. "We know about the demon you deal with, but there's much about the process that's a mystery. You and the others who have faced him keep it a secret. You don't let the rest of us benefit."

"We can't include you," Dervish says stiffly. "He deals with one case at a time, and only with those who have some experience of magic. That's how it works. It's not our choice — it's *his*."

"The demon," Prae nods. "Lord —"

"Don't say his name here," Dervish stops her. "It's dangerous."

Prae looks around nervously. I feel the hairs rise on the back of my neck. Then Dervish catches my eye and tilts his head ever so slightly. It's a gesture I know well — he does that sometimes instead of winking. I realize he's winding Prae up, giving her a scare. I hide a smile behind my hand and wait for her to settle down.

"It's not fair," Prae resumes, less composed than before.

"We've never had any contact with the demon. Maybe we could strike our own deal if you put us in touch with him."

"You couldn't."

"But you should let us try. We —"

"We've had this conversation before," Dervish interrupts. "We're not having it again. The Lambs follow the path of science. Demons are creatures of magic. The two don't mix. End of story."

"Very well," Prae says, showing open anger for a second, her pale face flushing. "You choose to lock us out — there's nothing we can do about that. But it means we don't know all that we should about the cure. We have no proof that it works in the long term, or why. So it's natural for us to be suspicious, to run our own checks, to be safe."

"Totally natural," Dervish says sarcastically. "But I don't think you'd have waited until now to make sure Billy wasn't killing. If you were checking on him prior to his change, I'm sure you've monitored him in the year-plus since. So your first reason for being here is a crock — you know Billy's fine. Let's move on to reason two, and try to make it a bit more believable this time."

Prae glares at Dervish, then glances at me. "*Two*," she growls. "We wanted to check on Grubbs. He's at a dangerous age. Both his brother" — my stomach tightened another notch. She knows about Bill-E!— "and sister turned. We thought it advisable to have a look at him. We kept out of the way while you were . . . indisposed, but now that you're back on your feet, we felt it was a good time to have a chat." She faces me and smiles. "How have you been sleeping lately?

Any bad dreams? Woken up with dirt under your finger-nails or —"

"You know what she's doing, don't you, Grubbs?" Dervish asks.

"Trying to freak me out," I mutter edgily.

"Correct. If they wanted to check up on you, they'd do it secretly. You'd never know they were there. She's saying this to upset you, because I've upset her. So ignore it. And you," he says to Prae. "Tell me the real reason you're here, or get the hell out."

"Very well." Prae stares at Dervish challengingly. "We want to run some test on Billy under laboratory conditions."

"You want to turn my nephew into a guinea pig?" Dervish laughs harshly. "You want me to sign him over, so you can prod and poke him and have him urinate into a cup at your command?"

"It's not like that. We —"

"Get out!" Dervish shouts.

"You're being unreasonable," Prae objects. "You haven't let me finish."

"Oh, you're finished," Dervish laughs. "I've heard enough. Now march back out to your car and —"

"Have you seen a child who's turned?" Prae asks me, rais-ing her voice. "You must have seen your brother, but only in the early stages of his transformation. It takes a few months for the disease to properly set in. They grow hair. Their fea-tures distort. Their spines twist. I have some photographs that —"

"No!" I shout. "I don't want to see any photos. I've seen them before."

"Children your own age," Prae says quickly as Dervish stands and strides towards her. "Some even younger. We have an eight-year-old girl. Her parents didn't know about the curse. She killed her mother. Chewed her throat open and —"

"You're so out of here," Dervish snarls, reaching to grab Prae's collar.

"Wait." I stop him, holding up a hand.

"Grubbs, don't listen to —"

"Just wait a minute. Please?"

Dervish breathes out heavily, then takes a step back.

"We're trying to help," Prae says, speaking to me but looking at Dervish. "Your uncle is a man of old science — he calls it magic, but to us it's science by a different name. We're of the new school. Dervish fights one battle at a time. Your mother and father made that choice too. But we're trying to attack the root of the disease. We want everyone to benefit, not just a few. To do that, we have to examine and explore.

"Your brother is one of the very few victims to beat the curse. If we can study him, unlock the secrets behind his remarkable cure, perhaps we can replicate it and save others — without the need for demons or so-called magic."

"You can't," Dervish says wearily. "I've told you before, it's *not* science. It's not of this universe. You can't understand it and you can't mimic it. Do you think I'd stand in your way if I thought there was the slightest chance that you could?"

"You can't be sure," Prae says.

"I am."

Prae mutters something beneath her breath, then tries

me again. "We wouldn't hurt Billy. You and your uncle could come and observe. We just want to know more, to understand . . . to help."

I feel sorry for Prae Athim. Despite her scary appearance and manner, she only wants to do good. But the thought of her taking Bill-E away, locking him up, experimenting on him . . . I shake my head.

"You should leave now," Dervish says quietly. "We can't help you."

"You're condemning others to change, to die," Prae says angrily.

Dervish shrugs. "We've been condemned a long time. We're used to it."

He lays a hand on Prae's shoulder. She jerks away from him and stands. "My daughter changed," she hisses. "I tried to cure her, but I couldn't. She's still alive. Because I hope and believe. By denying us, you deny her, and all the others like her. How will you sleep with that on your conscience?"

"Lousily," Dervish says. "But Billy will sleep sweetly. And to me, that's what matters most, just as your daughter matters most to you." He leans towards her. "If the positions were reversed, would you allow *your* loved one to be taken?"

"Yes," Prae answers immediately. "Without question."

"Well, that's where we differ. Because I always question."

"There are other ways," Prae says, a dangerous tremble to her tone. "We didn't have to ask. We could just take him."

Dervish's expression goes dead. "Try it," he whispers. "See what happens."

"You couldn't stop us," Prae insists, a red flush of anger

rising up her throat. "You're powerful, but so are the Lambs. We could —"

"Mess with me and you mess with us all," Dervish interrupts. "Do you really want to do that? Do the Lambs now think themselves the equals of the Disciples?"

"We aren't afraid of your kind," Prae says, but her words ring hollow.

Dervish smiles lazily. "If you lay a hand on Billy or Grubbs, I'll teach you to be afraid. That's a promise."

"You don't want us as enemies," Prae warns him. "Nobody stands alone in this world, not even the Disciples. You may need us one day."

"Yes," Dervish agrees. "But not today." He points at the door.

Prae opens her mouth to try again. Realizes she'd be wasting her breath. Shakes her head with disgust. Shoots a look at me. "Pray you never turn. Because if you do, thanks to people like your uncle, we won't be able to help. All we'll be able to do is kill."

She strides to the door, throws it opens, and marches out. The front doors slam several seconds later. Then the faint sound of her engine starting, rising, fading.

Dervish stares at me. I stare back. Neither of us says anything. I don't know what my uncle's thinking, but there's only one glaring thought in my head — who the hell are *the Disciples*?

MONSTERS GALORE

✠ ✠ ✠

DERVISH has another nightmare. Four nights in a row —
he must be going for a record. Luckily I'd been expecting
this one. Dervish shut himself off from me after Prae Athim
left. Kept to his study, pacing around, muttering, brooding.
I guessed nightmares would follow. Stayed awake after he
went to bed, alert, prepared for a long, active night.

I catch Dervish in the hall of portraits. He snuck past my
room without me hearing, even though I'd been listening
closely. But a minute ago the screaming started, and it was
easy to track him down.

The walls of this hall are lined with photographs and
paintings of dead family members, mostly teenagers who became werewolves. It's on the first floor, close to my bedroom. When I arrive, Dervish has knocked several photos to
the floor and is wrestling with a large portrait, trying to tear
it free of its peg.

"Leave me alone!" he screams. "It's not my fault!"

"Dervish," I call, hurrying over to him, grabbing his right

hand, trying to pry his fingers loose. "Derveeshio! Derv on a curve — don't lose your verve. Don't roar and bawl — not in this hall."

He ignores the rhymes and jerks free. "You're eating my brain!" He collapses to his knees, grips his head hard with both hands, moans with pain and terror.

"Dervish, easy, it's OK, it's coolio, you have to chill. You on the ground — everything's sound."

His eyes fix on a nearby photograph. His breath catches. "I didn't do it!" he gasps. "I didn't kill you! Leave me alone!"

I sweep the photos away, then grab Dervish's hands, pull them down from his head, and lock gazes with him. "Wake up, you crazy bald coot! It's only a dream — no need to scream. None of it's real — fantasy's the deal. You have to snap back. Come on, I know you're in there, I know . . ."

His expression clears. He looks like a lost child for a few seconds, pitiful, silently begging me for help. Then the real Dervish surfaces and terror gives way to exhaustion and embarrassment. I release him, nodding slowly and repeatedly to show that everything's OK, no damage done.

Dervish looks around at the photos on the floor. Most are ripped, a couple beyond repair. No glass in the frames. We removed all the glass a few months ago, in case something like this happened. Didn't want him hurting himself — or me.

"I thought they'd come back to life," Dervish says. "They blamed me. Claimed I was the cause of the curse. They wanted revenge."

"It was just a dream."

"I know. But still . . ." He shivers. "I could have done

without Prae Athim and the Lambs. I didn't need them now. Not in this state. Why do bad things always come at the worst time?"

"Forget about her," I tell him. "She's gone. You ran her off."

"Maybe I shouldn't have. Maybe . . ." He coughs, then stands. "No. That's the nightmare talking. The Lambs can't help. They mean well, but in matters like this they're helpless."

"Unlike the Disciples?" I ask, broaching the mysterious subject for the first time, not sure if it's the right moment, but curiosity getting the better of me.

Dervish shakes his head. "I'll tell you about them later. Not now. OK?"

I sniff like it doesn't matter.

Dervish grows thoughtful. "Billy doesn't know about the change, Lord Loss, what we did for him. It's better this way. No point throwing his world into chaos. The Lambs are part of the human world. They've no direct experience of the Demonata or magic. They couldn't learn anything from Billy."

"Then don't worry about it," I mutter. "Go back to bed, get a good night's sleep, kick the nightmares out the window."

Dervish laughs. "If only it was that easy." He checks his watch. Yawns. "But I'll try to snooze, to keep nurse Grub-bitsch happy." He glances at me. "If I drop off, I might go walking around again. You should lock me in."

"Nah," I smile. "You'd wreck the room. Don't worry about it. I'll sleep with one ear open. I'll see you don't come to harm."

Dervish reaches over, squeezes my hand, then shuffles off for the stairs and bed. I watch until he turns the corner. Stay for a while, thinking about Bill-E, the Lambs, demons, the mysterious Disciples. Then I start clearing up the photos and hanging the less tattered snapshots back on their pegs, knowing I won't be able to sleep.

✠ Tired. Finding it hard to stay awake. My friends want to know if there are any David A. Haym updates, but I only grunt at their questions. Studying Bill-E during lunch. Thinking about him in the hands of the Lambs, strapped to a table, hooked up to banks of electrodes. Can't let that happen. I faced Lord Loss for my brother. If Prae Athim tries anything with Bill-E, she won't just have to worry about Dervish and the Disciples — she'll have to deal with me.

Yeah, I know, she's hardly trembling with terror at the thought of having to go up against a teenager. But I'm big. And I can be nasty. If I have to.

✠ A limousine's parked in the driveway when I get home. A chauffeur sits behind the wheel, dozing. No prizes for guessing who the limo belongs to.

I hear her as soon as I push open the front doors. She's in the TV room. A loud voice, high-pitched, very theatrical. She's talking about one of her earlier movies — it might be *Zombie Zest* — telling Dervish about the problems she faced trying to get the look of the monsters right.

". . . but *every*body's using CGI these days! I don't like it. The audience can tell. They're not afraid. It's psychological. You see a guy in a monster costume, or a cleverly designed puppet, and even though you *know* it's not real, you can trick yourself into believing it is. But if you see something that's the work of a computer, your brain can't accept it. It doesn't scare you. I think . . ."

I walk into the room and cough softly. Davida Haym looks up from where she's sitting on the couch. A surprisingly normal-looking woman. Fiftyish. Black hair streaked with grey. Pudgy. A warm smile. Purple-rimmed glasses. A bright, flowery dress. She looks more like a giggling granny than a horror movie meister.

"Davida, this is my nephew, Grubbs," Dervish introduces us. He's sitting beside her on the couch, looking a bit over-whelmed — I have the feeling Davida hasn't stopped talk-ing since she came in. "Grubbs lives with me."

"Hello, Grubbs," Davida says, rising to shake my hand. A short woman. Barely comes up to my chest. "Neat name. Is it short for something?"

"Grubitsch," I mutter. "I'm a big fan of yours. I thought *Night Mayors* was the best horror film of the last ten years."

"Why, thank you!" Davida booms, not releasing my hand. "Although, to be honest, my input wasn't so great. The di-rector — Liam Fitz — is a real hardhead. Likes to make the creative decisions himself. I set him free, gave him what-ever he asked for, but after that . . ." She shrugs, still holding my hand.

"And this is June," Dervish says, drawing my attention to a third person in the room, sitting in a chair to my left.

"Juni," she corrects him, getting up. "Juni Swan." Davida Haym finally releases my fingers and I shake hands with the other woman. She's small too, but slightly taller than Davida. Thin. Pretty. White hair, very pale skin, pinkish eyes. An albino. Her hair's tied back in a ponytail. Hard to tell her age, because her skin's so white and smooth.

"Juni is Miss Haym's assistant," Dervish says.

"Davida," the producer corrects him. She tuts loudly. "I don't stand on ceremony."

"And I'm not her assistant," Juni says, almost apologetically. She speaks very softly. "Although I am here to assist."

"Let's sit down," Davida says, as if this was her house. She leads us back to the chairs and pats the space on the couch beside her, forcing me to sit with her and Dervish. "I've been telling your uncle about my problems on my other movies. As I'm sure you know — I can tell you're a horror buff — I *love* monsters. *LOVE* them! Fangs, tentacles, bulging eyes, slime . . . all great stuff, right? Right! But getting them to look real . . . believable . . . scare people to the max . . . that's hard as hell. But I'm telling you nothing new. You've seen loads of terrible monster flicks, I'm sure. Where the creatures are about as scary as a baby in a stroller?"

"Right," I grin. "Most horror films are crap. That's why they're fun."

"I agree!" Davida shouts. She thumps Dervish's knee so hard that he gasps. "I like this kid! He knows his thorns from his roses!" She turns back to me. "We all love schlocky horror, where the effects are lame and the monsters tame. I grew up on old Universal and Hammer pictures! And that's fine. Sometimes you just want to sit down to a corny bit of hokum and have a laugh."

She raises a finger and lowers her voice. "But there are times when you don't want to laugh, right? When you want to be scared, when you want your world turned upside down, when you want to sit there in the dark and really feel fear *bite*. Right?"

"Hell, yeah!" There was a period, after my battles with

Lord Loss and his familiars, when I didn't enjoy horror. Life was fearful enough. But as the months passed, and the memories of the real horror faded, I rediscovered my love of fictional terror.

"That's where I want to go with my next movie," Davida says, loud again. "I've been off the scene for a while — almost four years since my last film. That's because I've been researching and planning. I want to do something *big* with my next one, not rehash an older story. I want screams, not laughs. I want to go for the jugular and shake audiences up, send them home shivering."

"Coolio!" I exclaim.

"Which is where your uncle comes in." Davida smoothes down her skirt and turns her smile on Dervish. "Will we talk business now or do you want to wait?"

"Now's good for me," Dervish says.

"OK." Davida glances around, to be sure nobody's eavesdropping. "I'm about to shoot my new film. Everything's set. I'm not only producing — I've written the script and I'm directing too. Can you imagine? *Me* — a director!" She throws her head back and laughs. Dervish and I laugh too, even though we've no idea what the joke is.

"I've kept the project secret," Davida continues. "I keep quiet about all my films, but I've been especially hush-hush on this one. Everyone connected signed a lips-sealed contract. The monster designs are locked in a state-of-the-art safe, and only two other people besides myself have seen them in their entirety — everybody else gets a small piece to work on. We won't be shooting in any of the established studios. I've created my own, far away from prying eyes. Most people aren't even aware that I'm at work again — they think I'm sitting on my ass on a beach, twiddling my thumbs, creatively defunct."

"Sounds like you've given yourself a lot of headaches," Dervish says.

"Are you kidding?" Davida snorts. "I'm having a ball! It's the film I've always wanted to make. I love intrigue, suspense, secrets. It's a game, the best in the world, and I'm the only one who knows all the rules. I wouldn't trade places with anybody right now, not for anything."

"I'm glad you're happy," Dervish says. "But I don't see why . . . ?" He leaves the question hanging.

"Why I'm telling *you*." Davida looks at me and winks. "Why I'm telling the *two* of you." She lowers her voice again. I don't think she's capable of whispering, but this is as close as she gets. "What I say now has to remain between us. I haven't asked you to sign a confidentiality form yet — you'll have to do it later, if you agree to my offer — but from what I've heard, you're a man of your word. I'm not sure about Grubbs . . ."

"I can keep a secret," I huff. "You don't have to worry about me."

"Excellent." She gives my right knee a squeeze and almost crushes it. "So, when I ask you to keep what I'm about to say to yourselves, not tell anybody, even your best friends . . . can I trust you?"

"I won't speak, even under torture," Dervish laughs.

"Me either," I back him up.

"Great!" Davida beams. "Then listen close and keep it quiet. The film's called *Slawter*."

"*Slaughter!*" I echo. "Brilliant!"

"I think so too," Davida chuckles. Slawter — which is spelled wiht a 'w' instead of a 'ugh' — is the name of the town in the movie. A bit obvious, maybe, but I've always liked a gruesomely over-the-top play on words. I think it'll look great on the posters — 'Welcome to Slawter!' or 'Let the Slawter commence!'" She squints. "Maybe we'll have to work on the tagline, but you get the picture. Now, here's the good part, the reason I'm here, and the bit I know you're going to love the best. *Slawter* is going to be all about . . . *demons!*"

She sits back, grinning, and awaits our response, unaware that she's just dropped the mother of all bombshells.

✜ Davida can't understand why we're not excited. Doesn't know what to make of our shifty glances and awkward silence. She keeps talking about the movie. Tells us that demons take over the town of Slawter. She describes some of the characters and scenes. Dervish and I listen stiffly.

"OK," Davida finally says, "what's wrong?" She sniffs at her armpits. "Do I stink?"

Dervish forces a thin smile. "There's nothing wrong. It's just . . . We're not fond of demons, are we, Grubbs?"

"No," I grunt.

"Why not?" Davida asks. "Demons are the scariest monsters of the lot."

"Too scary," Dervish mutters, then laughs edgily.

Davida frowns. "But you're supposed to be a demon expert. The more I research, the more your name crops up. I've been told you know all about their ways, their habits, their appearance."

"You're talking about them as if they were real," Juni Swan chuckles.

"Of course they're not *real*," Davida snorts. "But there have been loads of stories and legends about demons, plenty of descriptions and paintings, and Dervish knows more about them than most. He has some of the hardest-to-find demonic books and manuscripts in the world. Right?"

"I know more than many, not as much as some," Dervish answers cagily. "What I can say is, demons aren't to be taken lightly. If you want to make stuff up, go ahead, use your imagination, have fun. But I suspect you want to do more than that."

"Damn straight," Davida huffs. "I want the real deal, the fiercest demons on record. I want this to be believable. I've got most of what I need — as I said, I've been working on this for four years. My demons are ready to go. But I want them to behave realistically. I want to get every last detail right, so even the greatest demon scholar won't be able to find fault."

Davida points at Dervish. "That's where *you* come in. I want your expertise, your insight and knowledge. I want you to come on set as an adviser. Tell us when we make mistakes, suggest different ways we might stage the demon scenes, help us pin the images down."

"You've got the wrong guy," Dervish says. "I don't do movies."

"There's a first time for everything," Davida insists. "I'm not saying you look on this as a career move — just a break from the norm. You get to see a film being made . . . hang out with the actors and crew . . . tell us what to do when we're messing up . . . and the money's not bad either!"

Juni coughs politely. "Davida, have you *seen* this place? I don't think money is an issue. Correct, Dervish?"

"I have to admit, I'm not hard up," Dervish says, smiling at Juni.

"So don't do it for the money," Davida shrugs. "Do it for the experience. You can bring Grubbs along too, if you wish. You'd like to see a movie being made, wouldn't you, Grubbs?"

"You bet!" I reply enthusiastically. Then I remember what the film's about. "But demons . . . they're . . . it sounds silly, but . . ." I make a face.

"This is incredible," Davida snaps. "I thought you guys would be dying to get in on this. There are others I can ask if you're going to be ridiculous about it. I'm not —"

"Davida," Juni interrupts calmly. "You won't convince them to get involved by antagonizing them. If they don't want to do it, you'll have to accept their decision and move on."

"I know," Davida mutters. "I just don't get why they're turning me down!"

"It's nothing personal," Dervish says, then looks at Juni. "What's your role in this, Miss Swan?"

"I'm a psychologist. There are lots of children involved in this movie. I've been hired to look after them on set."

"Do you do a lot of this type of work?" Dervish asks.

Juni shakes her head. "This is my first time."

"I brought Juni along because we're going to interview a young actor later," Davida says. "I like her to be involved with the kids as early as possible. She can spot a problem child a mile off."

"What about problem adults?" Dervish asks.

"I don't think you'd be any problem," Juni responds with a shy smile.

"I'm not so sure about that," Davida grumbles. Then she suddenly turns the full force of her smile on Dervish. "Dammit, Grady! I don't care if you're a problem or not. I want you on my team. What can I do to convince you?"

Dervish starts to say there's nothing she can do, then hesitates, glances at Juni, and frowns. "Do you have a copy of the script?"

"No," Davida says. "And I wouldn't show it to you if I did. But I've got some excerpts on a DVD, along with a rough plot outline and descriptions of some of the demons — I needed *something* to grab the interest of potential investors. But I don't like revealing even that much, especially to someone who hasn't signed a contract yet."

"I understand," Dervish says. "But if I could have a look, I'd be able to tell you whether or not you need me. I don't want to waste your time or mine. If there's no reason for me to be there — nothing I can help you with — then . . ."

Davida doesn't look happy. "I have a few copies of the DVD," she says, nodding at her handbag on the floor. "They're digitally protected, so you shouldn't be able to copy the material or send it to anyone by e-mail. But . . ."

She thinks it over, then reaches into the bag and produces a boxed DVD. "I don't know why I'm trusting you with this. You're not *that* important to me. But you're the first person to turn me down on this movie, and I don't like it. People aren't supposed to say no to the fabulous Davida Haym." She laughs shortly, then rises.

"You can have it for twenty-four hours. Juni and I have that interview tonight. We'll be passing back this way tomorrow. We'll drop in to collect the DVD. I'll ask — just once — if you've changed your mind. If you don't want to do it, fine." She beams at Dervish, nods at me, then heads for the door like a person of noble birth.

Juni gets up, smiling. "She's a drama queen, isn't she?" she says when Davida is out of earshot.

"And then some!" Dervish laughs.

"But she's sweet," Juni says. "And a natural with the children. She treats them like a mother. Not a bad bone in her body, despite the horrible films she makes."

Juni starts for the door. Pauses. Looks at Dervish. "I hope you change your mind. I . . ." She stops, clears her throat, smiles quickly, and exits. Dervish hurries after her, to see the pair out. I remain in the TV room, staring at the DVD on the couch, sensing trouble of the very worst kind, though I'm not sure why.

DON'T GO DOWN
THE CELLAR!

✠   ✠   ✠

DERVISH is humming when he returns. "Nice people," he says.

"Especially Juni," I note drily.

"Yes." He picks up the DVD and looks at it silently.

"What made you change your mind?" I ask.

"I haven't," he says.

"But you're thinking about it, aren't you?"

"Yes. This is probably nothing to worry about, just a film-maker conjuring up the usual smorgasbord of hysterical fakes. But I got the feeling Davida knows too much for her own good. She wants the film to be realistic. Maybe she plans to dabble where she shouldn't, use old rites that might backfire. I'm a hard man to find. I'm worried that she was able to root me out. It makes me wonder what else she might know."

"So you want to check the plot and demon descriptions, make sure there's nothing questionable going on?" I ask.

Dervish nods. "Except, I got the impression you only agreed to think it over when Juni smiled at you."

"Don't be ridiculous!" Dervish protests. "She had nothing to do with it."

But by the strength of his reaction, and the way he storms out of the room in a huff, I'm sure she did!

✛ Having shrugged off my foolish sense of unease, I try convincing Dervish to let me have a look at the DVD — I want to know what a David A. Haym film looks like at this early stage. But he refuses and locks himself in his study. Back downstairs, I fall asleep on the couch. Wake sometime during the night, cold, shivering. Think about hauling myself up to bed, but I'm too lazy. Instead I grab a few pillows and stack them around me for warmth. Starting to drift off to sleep again when I suddenly snap wide awake.

Dervish is in trouble.

Not sure how I know — gut instinct. I slide off the couch, scattering the pillows, and race upstairs. Dervish isn't in his bedroom or study. Nowhere on the second floor. Or the first. I wind up back on the ground floor. A quick search — no sign of him. That means he either went out . . . or down to the cellar.

Before descending, I go to the kitchen and make sure Dervish hasn't broken into the cutlery cupboard and stocked up on knives. Then I head down the stairs, automatic lights flickering on as I hit the bottom steps. The cellar is where Dervish stores his wine. I don't come down here much. Nothing of interest for me.

Listening to the hum of the lights, watching for shadows,

trying to pinpoint Dervish's position. After a minute I take the final step and explore the rows of wine racks, fists clenched, anticipating an attack.

I don't find Dervish in the cellar. Search complete, I want to go back upstairs and try the area outside the house. But there's one place still to look. It's the last place I want to try — which makes me suspect that's where Dervish is.

One of the walls houses a secret doorway. I head for that now. It's covered by a giant wine rack, mostly containing normal bottles. But one's a fake. I find it and press hard on the cork with a finger. It sinks in. The rack splits in two, and both halves slide away from each other, revealing a dark, narrow corridor.

"Dervish?" I call. My voice echoes back to me, unanswered.

I start down the corridor, breathing raggedly. The halves of the wine rack slide back into place. I'm plunged into darkness. But it's temporary. Moments later, lights flicker on overhead, the glow just strong enough to see by.

The corridor runs to a secret underground cellar. It's where Dervish keeps his most magical and dangerous books, where he goes if he wants to practice magic. It's where we fought Lord Loss all those months ago. Where I almost died.

I come to a thick wooden door with a gold ring for a handle. The door stands ajar, and there's a pale light coming from within. "Dervish?" I call again. No answer. I *really* don't want to go in, but I have to.

I push the door all the way open and enter, heart pounding.

A large room. Wooden beams support the ceiling. Many

torches set in the walls, but none are lit. A steel cage in one corner, the bones of a deer lying on the floor within. Two broken tables. A third in good repair. Chess pieces, books, charred pages, and other bits of debris brushed up against the walls. A stack of weapons close to the rubbish, lined with dust, riddled with cobwebs.

And Dervish, squatting in the middle of the room, a candle in one hand, a book in the other.

I approach cautiously. Freeze when I catch sight of the book. There's a painting of Lord Loss on the cover. Just his face. And it's *moving*. His awful red eyes are widening, his lips spreading. Dervish is muttering a spell, bending closer to the book. Lord Loss's teeth glint in the light of the candle. His face starts to come off the page, like a 3D image, reaching for Dervish, as though to kiss him.

I hurl myself at Dervish. Knock him over and punch the book from his hand. The candle goes out. We're plunged into darkness. Dervish screams. I hear him scrambling for the book. I thrash around, find Dervish, throw myself on top, and pin him to the floor, yelling at him, keeping him away from the book, calling his name over and over, using all my weight to keep him down.

Finally he stops fighting, pants heavily, then croaks, "Grubbs?" I don't reply. "You're squashing me," he wheezes.

"Are you awake?" I cry.

"Of course. Now get off before . . ." A pause. "Where are we?"

"The secret cellar."

"Damn. What was I . . . ?"

"You had a book about Lord Loss. You were chanting a

spell. His face was moving. It looked like he was coming alive — coming *through.*"

"I'm sorry. I . . . Let's get some light. I'm awake. Honest. You can get off me. I promise."

Warily I slide aside. Dervish gets to his feet. Stumbles to the nearest wall. I hear him rooting through his pockets. Then he strikes a match, finds the nearest candle, and sets the wick aflame. The room lights up. I see the book, lying facedown. No movement.

"Could you have brought him here?" I ask, not taking my eyes off the book.

"No," Dervish says. "But I could have summoned part of his spirit. Given him just enough strength to . . . hurt me."

"And me?"

"Absolutely not. You were safe. The spirit couldn't have gotten out of this room."

"But when I came in?"

Dervish says nothing. A guilty silence. Then a deep sigh. "Let's get out of here. There are things we must discuss."

"And the book?" I ask.

"Leave it. It can't do any harm. Not now."

Standing, I stagger away from the book, then out of the room. Dervish follows, leaving the candle burning, shutting the door on the past, trailing me back up the corridor to the safety of the normal world.

✠ "The Disciples fight the Demonata and do what we can to keep them out of our universe."

We're in Dervish's study. We both have mugs of hot chocolate. Sitting facing one another across the main desk.

"We're all magically inclined," Dervish continues. "Not true magicians, but we have talents and abilities — call us mages if you like. In an area of magic — the Demonata's universe, or a place where a demon is crossing — our powers are magnified. We can do things you wouldn't believe. No, scratch that — of course you'd believe. You fought Lord Loss."

"How many Disciples are there?" I ask.

"Twenty-five, thirty. Maybe a few more." Dervish shrugs. "We're loose-knit. Our founder is a guy called Beranabus. He *is* a true magician, but we don't see a lot of him. He spends most of his time among the Demonata, waging wars the rest of us couldn't dream of winning.

"Beranabus sometimes gives orders, assigns one or more of us a specific task. But mostly we do our own thing. That's why I'm not sure of our exact number. There's a core group who keep in touch, track the movements of demons, and work together to deal with the threats. But there are others we only see occasionally. In an emergency I guess Beranabus could assemble us all, but in the usual run of things we don't have contact with every member."

"So that's your real job," I say softly. "Fighting demons."

He smiles crookedly. "Don't misinterpret what I'm telling you. This isn't an organization of crack magical heroes who battle demons every week. There are a few Disciples who've fought the Demonata several times, but most have never gone up against them, or maybe only once or twice."

"Then what do they do?" I frown.

"Travel," he says. "Tour the world, watch for signs of demonic activity, try to prevent crossings in advance. Demons can't swap between universes at will. They need human assistants, wicked, power-hungry mages who work with them from this side and help them open windows between their realm and ours. Usually there are signs. If you know what to look for, you can stop it before it happens. That's what we do — watch for evidence of a forming window, find the person working for the demon, stop them before it gets out of hand."

"*You* don't travel around," I note. "Is that because of me?"

"No," Dervish smiles. "I used to travel a lot, but I do most of my work here now, at the command of Beranabus. It's my job to . . . well, let's not get into that. It's not relevant."

Dervish sips from his mug, looking at me over the rim, awaiting my reaction.

"What happens when a demon crosses?" I ask.

"It depends on the strength of the demon. Most of the truly powerful Demonata can't use windows — they're too big, magically speaking. They need a tunnel to cross — a wider, stronger form of window. They're much more difficult to open. It's been centuries since anyone constructed a tunnel."

"Lord Loss is a demon master," I note. "He crosses."

"He's an exception. We don't know why he can cross when others like him can't. He just can. There are rules where magic's concerned, but those rules can be bent. Anything's possible with magic, even the supposedly and logically *im*-possible.

"The other demons who cross are nowhere near as powerful as Lord Loss," Dervish continues. We drive back the lesser specimens, but we leave the stronger demons alone and just try to limit the damage."

"You let them get away with it?" I cry. "You let them kill?"

Dervish lowers the mug. It's not as heartless as it sounds. There's far less magic in our universe than theirs. When they cross, they're nowhere near as powerful as they are in their own realm. And most can only stay here for a few minutes. Occasionally a window will remain open longer, for an hour or two, but that's rare. Thankfully. Because if they could cross with all their powers intact, and stay as long as they liked, we'd have been wiped out long ago.

"We stop maybe half of all potential crossings," Dervish goes on. "Which is pretty good when you consider how few of us there are. Although we're only talking six or seven attempts to cross in any given year."

"So three or four get through?" I ask.

"More or less. We aren't always there when one crosses. When we are . . ." He sighs. "If it's a weaker demon, we try to drive it back. Usually a single Disciple will engage it, occasionally a pair. We don't like to risk too many in any single venture."

"And when you don't think you can stop it?" I ask quietly.

Dervish looks away. "A demon will normally kill no more than ten or twenty people when it crosses."

"Still!" I protest. "Ten *people,* Dervish! Ten *lives!*"

"What do you want us to do?" he snaps. "There are battles we can't win. We do what we can — we can't do any more. We're not bloody superheroes!"

"Sure," I say quickly. "Sorry. I didn't mean to sound critical. I just . . ."

"I know," he mutters. "When I first heard about the Disciples, I was like you. I didn't want to admit the possibility of defeat, or make concessions. But when you see enough people die, you realize life's not like the movies or comics. You can't save everyone. It's not an option."

Dervish falls silent. We never talked much about his past. To be honest, with all the problems I've faced over the last couple of years, I haven't had time to think about anybody else's troubles. But now that I consider it, I realize my uncle must have seen a lot of bad stuff in his time. We got lucky against Lord Loss. We beat him at his own game and walked away relatively unharmed. But Dervish told me there are more failures than successes when humans battle demons. And if he's been around for even a few failures . . . seen people die like I saw my parents and sister die . . . had to stand by and let it happen because he didn't have the power to stop it . . .

"I'm telling you this because of Davida Haym," Dervish says, interrupting my thoughts. "I went through her DVD earlier. From the outline it sounds like fun — demons run wild and take over a town — but I don't like it. The few demons she described are *very* realistic. She mentions rituals you can use to summon them. She's gathered information cleverly but I don't think she knows how dangerous that information is.

"I'm going to accept her offer to work on set as an adviser. I want to make sure she doesn't accidentally summon a demon or supply others with the means to. The chances of that happening are slim, and in the normal run of things I wouldn't bother with her.

"But I need to get away from here for a while." His eyes are dark, haunted. "I haven't been the same since I came back. The nightmares . . . fear . . . confusion. Maybe my brain will never properly recover, and I'm doomed to live like this until I die. But I'm hoping I can shrug it off. I've been living the quiet life — too quiet. I need something to focus my attention. A challenge. Something to sweep away the cobwebs inside my head."

"But you're protected by spells here," I note. "You might not be safe outside Carcery Vale. Lord Loss . . ."

"Remember the book in the cellar?" Dervish says. "Unless I dig myself out of this hole, I don't think I'm safe anywhere."

I nod slowly. "How long will you be gone?"

"However long the shoot lasts," Dervish says. "I'll ask Meera to keep an eye on things while I'm away."

"Meera's going to be staying with me?" I ask, not minding the sound of that one little bit — Meera Flame's hot stuff!

"No," Dervish says. "You won't be here either. Unless you object, I want to take you with me. Billy too."

"You want to take us on set?" I yelp.

"Davida said I could," he reminds me. "Well, she didn't mention Billy, but I'm sure that won't be a problem."

"Brilliant!" I gasp, face lighting up. Then doubt crosses my mind. "But why?"

"Two reasons," Dervish says. "One — I need you to look out for me at night, to help me if the nightmares continue." He stops.

"And the second reason?"

"I don't trust Prae Athim and the Lambs. They might pull a fast one if I'm not around."

"You think they'd kidnap Bill-E?"

"It's possible. Right now I want Billy where I can protect him, twenty-four seven. I'll rest easier that way."

"So we're going into the movie business," I laugh.

"Yep." Dervish laughs too. "Crazy, isn't it?" He checks his watch. "Three-thirty in the morning. Ma and Pa Spleen would hit the roof if we called Billy at such an ungodly hour." He cocks a wicked eyebrow at me. "Do you want to ring or shall I?"

PART TWO

✠ ✠ ✠

LIGHTS . . . CAMERA . . . DEMONS!

FILM FOLK

✠　　✠　　✠

"**I**'VE always wanted to eat human flesh. I mean, it's not an obsession or anything. I wouldn't go out of my way to kill, skin, and cook somebody. But I've always been curious, wondered what it would taste like. So, when the opportunity dropped into my lap, yeah, I took it. Does that make me a bad person? I don't think so. At least, not much badder than —"

"Worse than," Bill-E interrupts.

"*Worse!*" Emmet winces. "I keep tripping on that. 'Not much *worse* than, not much *worse* than, not much *worse* than . . .'"

I feel sorry for Emmet, watching him struggle to learn his lines. It's not easy to keep a load of words that aren't yours straight inside your head, then trot them out in a seemingly normal fashion. I used to think actors had a great life. Not anymore. Not after a week on the set of Slawter.

Slawter, as Davida told us when she visited Carcery Vale, is the title of the movie and the name of the fictional town that features in it. It's also what they've called the huge set that Davida's crew has constructed. It's an amazing place. They found a deserted town in the middle of nowhere. Rented the entire area and set to work restoring the buildings, clearing the streets of rubble, putting in fake streetlamps, telephone wires, signs for restaurants, hotels, bars, and so on. They also erected a lot of fake buildings that look real from the front but are entirely empty on the other side. Walking down the streets, it's hard to tell the real buildings from the fake ones — until you open a door.

There are trailers on the outskirts of Slawter — the movie veterans refer to them as the circus — where many of the cast and crew sleep, but a lot of us are staying in the old, real buildings. Since we're so far from any other town, Davida decided to turn some of the buildings into makeshift hotels, so everyone could stay in one place, in comfort. The "hotel" where Dervish, Bill-E, and I are staying looks like a butcher's shop out front, but it's cozy inside.

I've been told this isn't the way films are normally made. Usually the crew does a bit of location work, then heads back to the studio to shoot the interior scenes. But Slawter *is* the studio. There are huge warehouses, built beyond one end of town, where the interiors can be shot. And since all the outdoor action in the film is set in the town, everything can be done on-site. They even do the editing here, and the special effects. Often, on a big-budget film, there might be several teams around the world working on effects at the same time. But Davida wants to keep total control over this project. She refuses to farm out any of the work, even though it makes life much harder for her. This is her baby, the jewel in her movie crown, and she's doing it exactly the way she wants — damn the inconvenience!

She even insists on keeping the cast together for the duration of the shoot. Emmet's worked on a couple of films before, and explained how, if you have a small part in the movie, you only turn up for a few days, shoot your scenes, then head off. Even the big stars don't hang around the set the whole time.

Well, here they do. All the actors, cameramen, artists, carpenters, caterers — *everyone* — had to agree to stay here until filming is finished. Davida kept everything secret in the buildup to shooting. Now that we're all on set and the cameras are rolling, most of the secrets have been revealed. Copies of the full script have been circulated, and we've seen some of the demon costumes. To make sure none of the secrets leak to the outside world, Davida arranged for everyone to remain in Slawter until the entire film has been shot.

It costs a fortune to keep us here — food and drinks are free, games have to be organized to keep people amused in their spare time, two swimming pools have been built, tennis courts, a football field and so on — but Davida doesn't care. Her other movies made a ton of money, and she's managed to convince her backers that this one is going to be a mega-blockbuster, so she's free to spend whatever she likes.

Not having any jobs to do, Bill-E and I have been enjoying the filming. We wander through Slawter, watch scenes being shot, check out the old buildings and fakes, hang out with some of the other kids, and generally just have fun. It's great. Reminds me of when I first moved to Carcery Vale, when Bill-E and I spent pretty much all our free time together. We're best buddies again, breezing along in a little world of our own, no Loch Gossel or other friends of mine to complicate the situation.

You can divide the children of Slawter into three groups. There are the actors, twenty or so. Most don't have much experience, or have only been in a few films, like Emmet Eijit, who's our best friend here.

Then there are the actors' relatives. It's a big deal being a child actor. There are all sorts of rules and regulations. They can only work so many hours a day. They have to be tutored on-set. At least one of their guardians — normally a parent — has to be with them all the time. And there have to be other children for them to play with. Juni's in charge of that side of things. She makes sure the kids are being looked after, having fun, not feeling the stress of being part of such a costly, risky venture.

Finally there's the likes of Bill-E and me, children of people working on the film. Because everyone involved had to move to Slawter for the duration of the shoot — at least three months — they were allowed to bring their families. Davida likes the relaxed family atmosphere.

We don't have much personal contact with Davida Haym. Or with Dervish. He's been working closely with Davida since we arrived, advising, censoring, subtly guiding her away from the workings of real demons wherever possible. He's one of the few people to have seen inside the D workshops. That's where the demon costumes are being created. The demons are to be a mix of actors in costumes and mechanized puppets. There will be some CGI effects, but Davida's trying to keep the computer trickery to a minimum.

The costumes and puppets are housed in a giant warehouse, the biggest in Slawter, and access is granted only to a chosen few. Some of the costumes have been given a public airing, but most are still locked up within the D. Dervish said it's a maze of corridors and subsections in there. He's only been allowed into to a couple of rooms so far, but he's trying hard to gain access to the rest, to check out all the demonic details.

"I've always wanted to eat human flesh," Emmet says again, running through his big lines for the fiftieth time today. He plays a minor villain in the film, a kid who becomes a cannibal and works for the demons. He dies about a third of the way through, having been discovered by one of the heroes while eating the corpse of their headmaster.

Davida is shooting the film in sequence as much as possible, although, as on any movie, certain scenes from later in the script have to be shot early. Which means Emmet is getting to "die" a couple of weeks earlier than he should have. He's super-excited about it.

"This is my first death scene!" he raved yesterday. "Most kids don't get to die on-screen — how many films have you seen where a child bites the big one? And it's the first visible killing of the movie!"

Later, excitement gave way to nerves. He's been fussing ever since, worried he'll blow his lines or not be able to scream convincingly when the demon turns on him and rips him to pieces.

" 'At least, not much badder than' — Dammit! I did it again, didn't I?"

"Afraid so," I laugh.

"Play it cool," Bill-E advises, mimicking Davida's on-set mannerisms. He's been even more impressed by the whole movie-shooting experience than me. Now he wants to be a director when he grows up.

"*Cool!*" Emmet snorts. "That's easy for you to say. You're not the one up there on display."

"You know the lines," Bill-E murmurs, then laughs like Davida when she's trying to calm a nervous actor. "You probably know your lines better than anyone on the set, even Davida. You're a professional. They'll come when you're filming. And if not, who cares? Nobody gets it right the first time. And even if they do, Davida reshoots it anyway. You'll nail it the fifth or sixth time."

Bill-E's not exaggerating about the reshoots. Every scene is played out at least six or seven times, from various angles, the actors trying out different expressions and tones. Apparently this is common. Repetition is part and parcel of the filmmaker's life. I don't know how they stand it. I'd go crazy if I had to do the same thing over and over, day after day.

"He's quite the expert, isn't he?" Emmet remarks cuttingly.

"Hey, man, I'm just trying to help," Bill-E says, unruffled.

"For someone with no real experience, you certainly know a lot about it."

Bill-E laughs Emmet's criticism away. "I'm just calling it like I see it. If you'd rather I left, no problem. Come on, Grubbs, let's go and —"

"No!" Emmet pleads. "I'm sorry. I'm just all wound up. One last time, please. If I don't get it right, we'll quit and all go play foosball. OK?"

"OK," Bill-E says. "But don't forget — *cooooooolllllllll*."

Emmet shoots him an exasperated glance, then shares a grin with me. Focusing, he repeats his lines silently to himself, then tries them out loud and all too predictably blows them again. As soon as he breaks down, we drag him off to the foosball table and keep him there, though we can't stop him muttering the lines as he plays.

✠ Dinner with Dervish, Juni, and some others, in the ginormous catering tent at the heart of Slawter. Everybody talking at once, a nice buzz in the air. A mime artist signals to me that he'd like the salt and pepper. His name is Chai and he's a bit of a nutcase. He never speaks, although he's not mute. Apparently he's perfectly chatty when he's not working. But throughout the duration of a shoot, he keeps his lips sealed. It doesn't matter that he has a tiny part in the movie, and will only be filming for a few days. Chai considers himself a *method actor*.

"How are you two managing?" Juni asks Bill-E and me. "Enjoying yourselves?"

"Totally!" Bill-E gushes. "It's great. Incredibly invigorating and inspiring. I think I've found my calling in life."

"Not getting into any trouble, are you?" Dervish grunts.

"As if!" Bill-E smirks.

"I was discussing your situation with Dervish earlier," Juni says hesitantly.

Uh-oh! It's never good when an adult says something like that.

"I'm worried that you'll fall behind in your schoolwork," Juni goes on. "Things have been a rush lately — Dervish accepting our offer, bringing you two with him, a crazy first week of shooting. Tutoring arrangements have been made for the other children, but we overlooked you and Bill-E. I think it would be a mistake to let things continue as they are, and Dervish agrees, so . . ."

"No!" Bill-E cries dramatically. "You're going to stick us in a class? Say it ain't so, Derv!"

"It's so," Dervish laughs. "Juni's right. We're going to be here three months, maybe longer. If you go that length of time without classes, it'll mean repeating a year when we get back to Carcery Vale."

"You won't have to do full days," Juni promises. "We keep classes flexible, to fit in around shooting, so it'll be a few hours here, a few hours there, just keeping you in line with what your friends are doing back home. That doesn't sound so awful, does it?"

"Too bad if it does," Dervish interjects before we can reply, "because you don't have a choice."

"Slave driver," Bill-E mutters, but he's only pretending to be grumpy. We both knew this was coming. The freedom couldn't last forever.

Juni and Dervish start talking to each other again. Juni's been with my uncle most times that I've seen him recently, which is strange, since they can't have a lot of business together. Dervish is part of the inner technical circle, whereas Juni's job revolves around the children. There must be another reason why he's sticking to her like superglue, and I think I know what it is — good old-fashioned physical attraction!

It seems incredible. If someone asked me a week ago, I'd

have laughed and said the bald old grouch didn't have a romantic bone in his body. But something's stirring in the hidden depths of Dervish Grady. There's a gleam in his smile that was never there before. He's switched to a pungent new aftershave. His clothes are freshly ironed. He's even started combing the wisps of hair dotted around the sides of his head into place. There's no doubt about it — he's trying to impress the cute albino!

✠ Juni knows that Bill-E and I are friends with Emmet, so she places us in his class. All of the other students are actors. There's the Kane twins, Kuk and Kik, a boy and girl, small and slender, very alike in looks. They don't speak much to anyone, going off by themselves whenever there's a free period. They have big roles in the film, as eerie psychic twins.

Salit Smit is the main child star of *Slawter.* He's a bit older than the rest of us. A nice guy but not the brightest spark. He just smiles and nods a lot in class, not bothering to apply himself, convinced he's going to be the biggest movie draw since Tom Cruise.

I absolutely despise the other three. A clique of snobs, presided over by the dreadful Bo Kooniart, a girl who was born solely to annoy. She's been in a few commercials and thinks she's God's gift. Always dresses stylishly, like a model. Sucks up to Davida and anyone else with power and influence. Ignores the rest of us, treating us like simpletons or servants.

Her brother, Abe, is almost as bad. A scrawny, miserable excuse for a child. He's not an actor, but his father — the loud, obnoxious Tump Kooniart, a movie agent — insisted he be cast if they wanted to hire Bo. From the rumors, Davida resisted, but finally caved in and gave him a small part as a kid who raises the alarm when the demons are about to break through *en masse*. I don't think Davida gives way too often, so Tump must be good at his job. Which is just as well, because from what I've seen of Bo and Abe, they're awful at theirs!

The third mini-tyrant is Vanalee Metcalf. Her parents are multimillionaires. Too busy to waste time with their daughter on-set, so she came equipped with her own bodyguard-cum-servant, who glares at anyone who doesn't grovel at her feet.

Bo, Abe, and Vanalee took one look at Bill-E and me when we were introduced to them this morning, smirked at each other in a snide, superior way, and turned their noses up to let us know we weren't worthy of direct notice.

Our tutor is a sweet but nervous woman named Supatra Jaun. I can tell within ten minutes that she can't handle Bo and her posse. She lets them talk to each other while she's teaching and doesn't ever try to assert her authority. Sometimes she'll murmur, "Now, now, Bo, please pay attention," but without any real hope that the blond, ponytailed, stick-thin brat will obey.

Miss Jaun seems genuinely pleased that Bill-E and I have been added to her class, probably because we're polite and show some interest. She talks to us warmly, finds out what we've been studying, takes a few notes, and promises to bring us up to scratch in next to no time.

"I bet those dirtbags know a lot about scratching," Bo sniffs.

"Meaning?" I growl at her.

"Lice, you moron!" she screeches, and Abe and Vanalee burst out laughing.

"We've found our nemesis," Bill-E mutters in my ear, pegging it dead-on. "Hate her, Grubbs. Hate her good and proper."

"Does her character die in the script?" I ask Emmet.

"No," he says. "She ends up saving the town, along with Salit."

"A pity," I sigh.

"But she does fall into a pit full of demon manure at one stage," Emmet says, and my day lights right up.

✠ Our first session lasts two hours, a mix of history, biology, and math. Miss Jaun seems to be confident in all subjects — a smart cookie. Then an assistant director pops in and says they need Bo and Salit. Miss Jaun checks her watch, says we might as well all take a break, and asks those of us not involved in filming to return in an hour. It's certainly a lot more laid-back than our school in Carcery Vale.

Emmet wants to practice his lines on Bill-E and me again, but we don't have the patience, so we leave him with his mom in his trailer. We grab sandwiches from one of the many mobile cafeterias, then go see if anything exciting is happening. There's not much to keep us amused today. Davida and her crew are setting up a tracking shot on a street, trying to get lots of actors in place and working in sync with each other. Fairly boring to watch. A lot of filming is.

"I still can't believe we're here," Bill-E says as we wander around. "Maybe this will become Dervish's full-time job and we'll travel around the world on film shoots with him."

"I doubt it," I laugh. "Your gran and grandad wouldn't allow it. I'm surprised they agreed to let Dervish have you for this long. Did he work some magic spells on them?"

"Nope," Bill-E says. "They were happy to let me come. Gran loves movies, especially old flicks starring the likes of David Niven and Ingrid Bergman. She thought this was a great opportunity for me. I think she's hoping I'll fall in love with a beautiful blind cellist or some such nonsense. She believes that a lot of those old films were based on true stories, that the world's really like that."

"Mind you, a girl would have to be blind to fall in love with you," I comment. "Otherwise they could never return your love, could they?"

"Your face," Bill-E snorts. "My flabby nether regions. Spot the similarity?"

I get Bill-E in a headlock and rub my knuckles into his skull, but it's all in fun. He has no idea of the real reason why he's here. He thinks Dervish is his father, that he didn't want to spend a few months parted from his darling son. He doesn't know about Dervish wanting to make sure Davida doesn't raise hell, or about Prae Athim's interest in experimenting on him.

"I can't wait to see the demon tomorrow — or it might even be tonight," Bill-E enthuses once I've released him. "Emmet says it depends on how shooting goes today. If they finish that shot on the street in time, they'll do his scene later. It'll be coolio!"

"Hmmm," I say neutrally.

"What are you moaning about, Goliath?" Bill-E frowns. Then, studying me carefully, his expression clears. "Oh. I'd forgotten. Your parents and sister . . ." He trails off into silence. Although Bill-E doesn't know about his lycanthropic genes, or the battle Dervish and I fought with Lord Loss, he knows that demons killed my family.

"Are you going to be OK with all this?" Bill-E asks awkwardly. Sympathy isn't something that he does well.

"Sure," I grunt.

"Really?" he presses. "Because they can't keep us here. I know Dervish signed those contracts saying we'd stay until the end, but *we* didn't. If you want to leave, there's nothing they'll be able to do about it. I've watched a lot of courtroom movies. I know what I'm talking about."

"No," I smile. "I'll be OK. I mean, we're talking movie demons here — rubber, wire, and paint. How scary can they be?"

✠ Emmet's nervous all afternoon, practicing his lines even in class. Davida popped in to see him during lunch and told him they'd definitely be shooting his death scene tonight. The way he's behaving — pale, shivering, mumbling to himself — I think it might take quite a few attempts to get it right!

Near the end of class, Emmet's summoned to the makeup trailer. He won't be required on-set for a few hours yet, but they want to run some tests. It's going to be a gory scene — Davida wants blood spurting every which way — so they need to make sure everything's set up smoothly before they stick him in front of the cameras.

Salit and Bo return as Emmet's leaving. "I can't believe they're letting you go through with this farce," Bo says, blocking the doorway. "You'll choke, Eijit. You know it, I know it, everybody knows it. So why don't you just —"

"Leave him alone!" Bill-E shouts. "Meddling cow!"

"Now, Billy-E, that's not —" Miss Jaun begins.

"Shut up, pipsqueak!" Bo defends herself, spitting venom at Bill-E. "If I want advice from a fat geek with a lazy eye, I'll let you know. Otherwise . . ."

I stand up, flexing my muscles, stretching aggressively. "You're going to apologize," I tell Bo flatly.

"Says who?" she retorts, but I've unnerved her. It's not often that I threaten anyone, but when I do, I can make quite an impression.

I step out from behind my desk and crack my knuckles, staring at Bo levelly. "*Now,*" I say firmly.

Bo glares at me, then sneers and says mockingly, "I'm so sorry, Billy one-eye. I won't point the truth out to you again." Her gaze flicks back at Emmet. "But you're still going to mess up. Let me know when you do. It's not too late for Abe to step in and do the job properly."

"Ignore her," Bill-E says, his left eyelid fluttering furiously. "You'll be great. Davida wouldn't have picked you if she didn't believe you could do it."

"Thanks," Emmet says hollowly, then pushes past Bo, visibly upset. Bo smirks and takes her seat.

"That wasn't very nice," Miss Jaun says disapprovingly.

Bo looks up at our teacher as though just noticing she's there. "Excuse me?"

"You shouldn't —" Miss Jaun begins.

"What was that?" Bo asks loudly, cutting Miss Jaun off. She tilts her head and pushes her lower lip out with her tongue, daring Miss Jaun to challenge her. For a moment it looks as though she will, and I ready myself to cheer the timid teacher on. But then her shoulders sag and she looks away.

"Let's get on with our lessons," she says meekly. "I'll finish up with the others, then take you and Salit for a couple of hours. Now, where were we . . . ?"

✠ "Someone should give it to her good," Bill-E storms when class has finished. "Bo freakin' Kooniart! Davida should put that little monster over her knee and spank her till her hand turns blue!"

"I agree," I say grimly, "but it's not going to happen. She's a star. She can get away with crap like that. To be honest, I thought they'd all be like her. I'm surprised how normal most of the others are."

"Too bad the demons aren't real," Bill-E grumbles. "We could feed Bo to them, and her horrible little brother. Vanalee too."

"It would certainly make life easier," I agree. "But they're not real. There's nothing we can do except ignore her. Come on." I slap his back. "Let's go see what Emmet looks like in his makeup."

✠ Emmet's covered in fake blood. He's spitting it out and wiping it from his eyes. "The bag exploded early," he moans.

"You squeezed too hard," a props person says, sliding a hand up inside Emmet's sweater, removing an empty plastic bag which had been filled with the red, sticky liquid. "You have to be more gentle. Don't worry — you'll get the hang of it soon."

Emmet goes off to be cleaned, before trying on a fresh costume and having his makeup applied again. Rather him than me. Sometimes an actor can spend most of the day sitting in a chair, having makeup dabbed on, cleaned off, dabbed on, cleaned off, dabbed . . .

Bill-E and I go for a swim, then head for dinner. We spot Dervish dining with Davida and Juni, but they're talking shop, so we don't disturb them. After that we check on Emmet again. This time he's managed not to burst the bag of blood and is ready to face the cameras.

"She's been trying to unsettle me all week," he says about Bo. "She thinks Abe should have had this part. Her dad does too. He told my mom I was an amateur and shouldn't be here."

"Charming!" Bill-E huffs.

"Mom hit the roof," Emmet chuckles. "Told Tump Kooniart what she thought of him and to keep out of our way for the rest of the shoot. She complained to Davida, but he's an agent for several of the actors, so there's not much Davida can do. In an argument, if it's us or him, she has to take his side. I could be replaced easily, but if Tump walked off and told his gang to follow . . ."

"Never mind," Bill-E says encouragingly. "There's nothing they can do about it now. This is your scene. Go out there, strut your funky stuff, and leave Tump Kooniart and his brats to stew."

Emmet laughs, then asks if he can run through his lines with us. This time we let him, and say nothing as he makes his customary mistake and grinds to a miserable halt. Then, before he can practice again, his call comes and we have to leave.

Showtime!

✚ This is the first big action shot of the movie, so a large crowd of curious bystanders has gathered. Thanks to modern technology, scenes with monsters aren't normally interesting to watch being filmed. More often than not, actors will play out their part against a blue screen background. The monster effects are added later, using computers.

But Davida wants the demons to look as lifelike as possible, for the action to play realistically. That means taking a less flashy approach than in her other movies, keeping it gritty and believable, using almost no computer effects.

Bill-E and I find a good place to watch, next to Dervish and Juni. The scene's being filmed on one of the smaller, darker alleys of Slawter. There's a manhole on the left side of the street, from which the cover has been removed. The demon will spring out of the manhole, grab Emmet, and drag him underground.

"This is going to be fun," Dervish says warmly. "Hardly anyone here has seen the demon costume. I think people will be really scared."

"Nonsense," Bill-E says. "How can you be scared of a guy in a monster suit?"

"Trust me," Dervish grins. "This doesn't look like a guy in a suit. There are engines and wires within the costume, so it can pull expressions, ooze slime like you wouldn't believe, even . . ." He lowers his voice. "It smells."

"Come again?" Bill-E blinks.

"Emmet doesn't know this, so don't say anything, but Davida wants to wring as much genuine terror out of him as she can. So she created a demon-type stench, to throw him off-guard. She has a few other tricks up her sleeve too. I feel sorry for the kid — he doesn't know what's going to hit him!"

"I don't think that's fair," I mutter. "He's nervous enough as it is."

"Don't worry," Juni smiles. "We talked it over with his mother. She gave us the all-clear. He'll enjoy the joke when he recovers. It will make the scene more believable, which will make his acting seem all the more professional. That will stand him in good stead when he's looking for his next big role."

I'm a bit worried about Emmet, despite Juni's reassurances. I'd hate if he got so freaked out that he couldn't finish filming the scene and had to hand the part over to Abe. I can see the moody Master Kooniart standing across from us, with Bo and their fat, leering father, Tump. I wonder if the stench idea was theirs to begin with.

I'd like to warn Emmet, but Davida is talking with him and Salit, explaining the dynamics of the scene. This is where Salit finds Emmet eating their headmaster, and realizes he's working for a demon. Emmet starts to give a long speech about how the demons are going to take over the town, and why he's working for them. In the middle of it, his demonic ally pops out of the manhole and makes off with him.

"It's important you don't look like you know what's going to happen," Davida tells Emmet. "As far as you know, this demon is your best buddy and Salit's the one in trouble. You'll hear some rumblings, feel a few tremors. Ignore them and concentrate on your lines."

"About that," Emmet cuts in. "I've been having a few problems."

"Oh?" Davida smiles and waits for him to continue.

"It's the line, 'At least not much worse than a guy who gives in to temptation and steals a candy bar.' I *know* the line, but I keep coming out with 'badder' instead of 'worse.' If it happens, can we do it again right away? I'll try to get it right, but I might . . ."

Davida holds up a hand. "Emmet, as far as I'm concerned, there's not one line in the script that isn't open to negotiation. I should have made that clear earlier. It's *your* voice I want to hear, not mine. If 'badder' is what comes naturally to you, then 'badder' it is."

"I can change the line?" Emmet gapes.

"Absolutely."

A big smile works its way across Emmet's face. Across from us, Abe and the other Kooniarts are glowering. They couldn't hear the conversation, but they can see the fear fade from Emmet. They've lost their chance to bump Abe up the pecking order. I want to thumb my nose at them and stick out my tongue. But that would be childish, so I settle for a smug wink when I catch Bo's furious eye.

They shoot the early scenes several times, from a variety of angles. A fake corpse is placed in the alley, close to the manhole cover. Emmet starts the scene crouched over it, pulling bits off and stuffing them in his mouth. He's so convincing, it's hilarious, and Salit keeps laughing when he comes upon him.

" 'Matt!' " he cries, calling Emmet by his screen name. " 'What are you doing with Mr. Litherland's nose in your . . .' Sorry!" he shouts, doubling over. "I can't help it! He looks so crazy!"

"Don't worry," Davida says, smiling patiently. "We have all night. Keep trying. The joke will wear thin eventually." She grimaces at a cameraman. "I hope!"

✠ Salit finally gets through his lines without laughing and they move on to the next scene. The cameras and lights are redirected, the makeup artists make sure Salit and Emmet are looking the way they should, Davida has a last few words with Emmet, then they're ready to go.

"OK, people," an assistant director yells. "We're going to try and get this right the first time, so we want *absolute* quiet!"

When everyone settles down, the technicians do their final checks, Davida looks around slowly from one member of the crew to another, then nods. A man calls out the title, scene, and take, and snaps the traditional clapperboard shut.

"And . . . action!" Davida roars.

"'How could you do it?'" Salit cries, in his role as Bobby Mint, boy-hero.

"'What?'" Emmet protests. "'It's not as if anyone liked Mr. Litherland.'"

"'But he's human!'" Salit cries.

"'He *was*,'" Emmet corrects him. "'He's yummy for my tummy now!'" Emmet rubs his stomach with a sick laugh. "'I've always wanted to eat human flesh. I mean, it's not an obsession or anything. I wouldn't go out of my way to kill, skin, and cook somebody. But I've always been curious, wondered what it would taste like. So, when the opportunity dropped into my lap, yeah, I took it. Does that make me a bad person? I don't think so. At least, not much badder than a guy who gives in to temptation and steals a candy bar. It's not like I killed him myself.'"

"'But you let it happen!'" Salit cries. "'You knew about the demon!'"

Emmet shrugs. "'What's done is done. No point crying over spilled milk — or a butchered headmaster.'" He holds out severed, bloodied arm to Salit. "'You should try some, Bobby. You might like it. It . . .'" The ground begins to rumble. A foul stench fills the air. For a second, Emmet falters and his gaze flicks to the open manhole. Then he recovers and continues like a true professional. "'It goes down super sweet, especially if you add a dollop of ketchup. Tastes a bit like —'"

That's when the demon bursts out of the manhole and grabs him.

It happens in a blur, and is so fast, so violent, so shocking, that several people in the crowd gasp.

The demon is green, slimy, with fierce yellow eyes, four long arms with claws at the ends, a mouth full of fangs. There's something wolfish about its face, long and lean, with patches of hair here and there.

The demon whips Emmet off the ground. He screams, not having to fake it, caught off-guard. Salit falls backwards, yelling with genuine horror.

My world goes red with fear. I'm thrown back in time . . . that night in the cellar . . . earlier . . . my old home . . . walking into my parents' bedroom to find Lord Loss, Vein, and Artery at work. Feeling the exact same thing in my gut now as I did then.

The demon screeches and vanishes back underground,

carrying Emmet with it. There's a moment of hush. Then Emmet's face appears, sheer terror in his expression. "Help!" he cries. "For the love of —"

Blood erupts around him, shooting up through the hole like a geyser. The howl of the demon drowns out his final words. His eyes go wide, then dead. As his head slumps, the demon pulls and Emmet disappears again, this time forever.

It all happened so swiftly, I'm in a state of shock. So is everybody else. Stunned silence. People with hands over their mouths and disbelief in their eyes. I sense screams building in a dozen throats, ready to erupt at once, a chorus of terror.

"Now that's what I call a death scene!" Davida Haym roars triumphantly, shattering the spell of fear. "Cut! Did you get that? You'd better have! We'll never top that take!"

And suddenly everybody's laughing, relief flooding through them. They thought for a few seconds that the demon was real, that Emmet was really being attacked. Now the moment has passed and they've remembered — this is make-believe, horrific fun, a movie. They're embarrassed at having been faked out, but since so many of the others reacted the same way, they're not left feeling *too* red-faced.

"I told you!" Dervish laughs, clapping loudly. "Wasn't that the most vicious, coolest thing you've ever seen?"

"My heart!" Juni gasps, fanning her face with one hand. "I didn't expect it all to happen so fast!"

"That was amazing!" Bill-E exclaims. "Did you see it all, Grubbs? That spray of blood — like it was coming from a fireman's hose! It was . . . Grubbs? Are you OK? Hey,

Dervish, I think there's something wrong with Grubbs. He looks like . . ."

I block out Bill-E's words and the other sounds. I experienced the same sense of terror that many of the people around me felt. The same jolt of fear. The same moment of belief that this was real. But whereas they've gotten over that moment, I can't.

Because I'm remembering the look of the demon. Its movements. The hate in its eyes. The effect it had on me.

And I'm staring at the open manhole cover, all the blood around it, no sign of Emmet or the monster.

And I'm thinking . . . every part of me is insisting . . .

That was no damn guy in a suit.

That demon was *real!*

THE LAUGHINGSTOCK

✤ ✤ ✤

"IT was just a movie monster," Dervish says.

"No. It was real. It killed Emmet."

We're still in the alley. The blood's being washed away, and people are chattering about the big scene with the demon. I grabbed Dervish as soon as I could move. Told him what I thought. He thinks differently.

"Grubbs, come on, I said it was going to be realistic. You're —"

"I know what I saw!" I retort, voice rising. "That was a demon, like Lord Loss! It killed Emmet!"

Juni looks at me oddly. Bill-E is gawping openly. Dervish smiles crookedly at them, takes hold of my elbow, and marches me out of earshot. "Are you insane?" he hisses as we turn a corner. "We're on a film set. That was a guy in a costume. A very convincing costume, but just —"

"Don't tell me you thought that wasn't real," I moan. "Didn't you feel it in your gut, the same thing you felt when we faced Lord Loss? The magic in the air?"

Dervish glares at me. Starts to say something. Stops, his expression softening. "I've been a fool. I thought you'd gotten over the Lord Loss incident, but I guess you haven't."

"Of course I haven't 'gotten over' it!" I snort. "You don't 'get over' demons murdering your parents and sister! But I've dealt with it. Moved on. This isn't delayed shock. I know what I saw, and that was a *real* demon."

"You're hysterical," Dervish says.

"No," I snarl. "Look at me. Look into my eyes. I'm not being a big kid. That. Was. A. Demon. Nobody can mimic the look and movements — the aura — of a real demon. I don't care how many special effects artists work on it. Some things can't be replicated, by anybody, ever."

"Grubbs . . ." Dervish can't think of anything else to add.

"Where's Emmet?" I challenge him. "If he was acting, why didn't he come out when Davida yelled 'cut'?"

"They took him away to wash the blood off," Dervish says.

I shake my head. "I bet you're wrong. I bet we can't find him."

Dervish sighs impatiently. "OK. Let's go look for Emmet. But!" He raises a finger. "When we find him, and you see that he's unharmed, I want you to accept it. I don't want you saying it's not really Emmet, it's a changeling, or any nonsense like that. OK?"

"Fine," I smile bitterly.

Grumbling sourly, Dervish leads me away in search of Emmet Eijit, even though I know in my heart that the only place we'll find him now is amidst the bones and scattered shreds of skin in some dirty demon's den.

✥ ✥ ✥

✥ Emmet's not in any of the trailers. Nobody has seen him. I shoot Dervish a meaningful look, but he waves it away and goes looking for Davida. She's still in the alley, talking with a technician. We wait for her to finish, then Dervish nudges forward and asks if she knows where Emmet is. Says we want to congratulate him on his performance.

"Of course!" Davida cries. "Hell, I want to too. I plain forgot about him. That was amazing. I loved the final touch — the scream for help. It worked perfectly. No need for a second take. He'll be getting the blood cleaned off, so —"

"No," I interrupt. "We checked. He isn't in makeup."

"Oh. Then I guess . . . Hey, Chuda! Where'd Emmet get to?"

A tall, thin man without eyebrows steps forward. Chuda Sool, the first assistant director and Davida's closest confidant. They've worked together on her last four films. He's a quiet sort, keeps to the background, makes sure everything's running smoothly, tries to head off problems before they bother Davida.

"There's been a flare-up," Chuda says softly. "Perhaps we should speak about it in private."

"What are you talking about?" Davida snaps. "What happened?"

"Nora — Emmet's mother — ran into Tump Kooniart after shooting," Chuda says. "They had a huge argument. Tump said some very nasty things. He upset her. Nora grabbed Emmet, demanded a car, collected their belongings and . . ." Chuda shrugs.

"They left?" Davida barks. "Are you mad? Nobody leaves until shooting finishes. It's in their contract. Get them back!"

"I can't," Chuda says. "When Nora calms down, maybe we can convince her to return, but —"

"She has no choice!" Davida barks. "She signed the contract. They have to stay on set for the duration."

"You're absolutely correct," Chuda says patiently. "But she went anyway. You can withhold Emmet's payment and maybe force them back that way, but for the time being . . ." He shrugs.

"Told you," I mutter, glancing up at Dervish. Then I turn and walk off, not wanting to waste my time on more ridiculous excuses. Emmet's dead, slaughtered by a demon. And if his mom's missing, that means she was probably killed too. Time for Grubbs Grady to make an ultra-quick exit from Slawter!

✠ "You can't just walk off," Dervish argues as I pack my bag.

"Watch me." I turn to Bill-E, who's standing by his bed, blinking like a startled owl. "You're coming too. I'm not leaving you to end up like Emmet."

"It looks bad, especially as there's no sign of Emmet," Dervish says. "But we need to make sure. Chuda could have been telling the truth. Emmet's mother —"

"Bull!" I snort. "There was no argument with Tump Kooniart. Chuda made that story up. Emmet was killed by a demon. His mom's dead too, I guess. Chuda must be working for the demon, since he lied to cover up the truth. And I doubt if he's the only one."

"Wait a minute," Bill-E splutters. "You believe that was a

real demon? You think Emmet was really killed? Are you crazy?"

"Maybe," I laugh shortly. "But if I am, I'm going to be crazy far, far away from Slawter. And you're coming with me. I won't leave you behind." I look hard at Dervish. "I *won't*."

"OK," Dervish sighs. "I won't keep you here against your will. But you're overreacting. Until we know for sure, we should —"

There's a knock at the door. Juni Swan. "Can I come in?"

I go stiff. Is Juni working with Chuda Sool and the demon? Has she been sent to convince me that my imagination has run wild? I like Juni. I'd hate to think that she's evil. But if she backs up Chuda's story . . .

"I wanted to check that everything's all right," Juni says, eyeing the bag that I'm in the middle of packing.

"Did Chuda send you?" I ask tightly.

"No. I came because I heard you telling Dervish that Emmet had been killed by a real demon. I wanted to know what you meant."

"I'd have thought that was obvious."

"You can't truly believe that was a real demon," Juni says. "Demons don't exist, do they, Dervish?"

Dervish clears his throat. "Well, I wouldn't say that, exactly. 'There's more in heaven and Earth, Horatio,' and however the rest of the quote goes."

"But . . . we're making a film about demons. That was just an act. Emmet —"

"— has mysteriously disappeared," I cut in.

Juni frowns. "Excuse me?"

"Nora had a fight with Tump Kooniart," Dervish explains.

"The way we heard it, she lost her temper, grabbed Emmet, demanded a car, and took off."

"But she can't have," Juni says. "Their contract . . . Nobody's allowed to leave until shooting wraps."

"They tore it up," Dervish says softly. "Allegedly."

Juni's frown deepens. Then she looks at me, expression clearing. "That explains the bag. You think this confirms what you suspected. You're getting out before the demons kill you too."

"Damn straight."

Juni nods slowly. "And if I try to convince you that Emmet hasn't been killed . . . that demons aren't real . . . would you think I was part of a conspiracy?"

I hesitate, not wanting to offend her if she's innocent.

"I don't know anything about a fight between Nora and Tump, or why Nora would have been allowed to leave," Juni says steadily. "And it's strange that it happened so quickly, without them saying goodbye to anyone. You might be right. The demon could have been real. Maybe it did kill Emmet."

Juni reaches inside the light jacket that she's wearing and pulls a pink cell phone out of a pocket. She holds it towards me. As I take it, suspicious, she says, "I have contact numbers for everyone connected to the children working on this film. Nora's number is in there. I'd like you to call her."

I glance up sharply. "No tricks," Juni says. "I don't know what will happen when you dial that number. I'm making no promises. I think Nora will answer, or if she doesn't, you can leave a message and she'll call back shortly. But short of us getting a car and tearing after them in hot pursuit, I think this is the only way to determine the truth."

I stare at the buttons. I don't want to do this. I want to pass the phone back to Juni, finish packing, and get the hell out.

But I can't. Because maybe — just maybe — I figured this wrong. Maybe the fear dates back to my fight with Lord Loss and my mind's playing tricks on me. I'm pretty sure it isn't. But if I refuse to dial Nora's number, I'll look like a crackpot.

I unlock the phone. Get to the list of names. "Is it under E or N?" I ask.

"N for Nora," Juni says.

I search for the Ns. There's a lot of them. I scroll down. There it is — Nora Eijit. I hit the send button. It rings. Once. Twice. Three times. Four. Fi-

"I don't want to talk about it!" a woman's voice snaps. "Kooniart can fry in the fires of hell! You tell him —"

"Mrs. Eijit?" I interrupt.

A pause. "Who's this?"

"Grubbs Grady. Emmet's friend."

"Oh. I'm sorry. I saw Juni's name come up, so I assumed . . ."

"I'm calling from her phone."

"I see. Do you want to speak to Emmet?"

"Yes, please." Speaking mechanically, figuring this could be any woman — I don't know Mrs. Eijit's voice well enough to make a definite identification. Waiting for the kicker, for her to say he's asleep, or he doesn't want to talk to me, or —

"I'll put him on."

The sound of her phone being handed over. The noise

of a car engine in the background. Then — Emmet. "Hi, Grubbs," he says quietly, miserably.

"Hi," I reply weakly.

"I can't really talk now. I'm sorry I split without saying goodbye. I'm hoping we can come back later, when —"

"No way!" Emmet's mom shrieks. "Not unless that fat fool Kooniart gets down on his knees and —"

"I'll have to call you back," Emmet says quickly and disconnects.

I look at the little red button on Juni's phone. Slowly, reluctantly, I press it. Hand the phone back to Juni. Raise my eyes. And smile like a fool, silently admitting to Juni and the others that I was wrong — even though, inside, part of me still insists the demon was real.

✠ "I can't believe you thought Emmet had been killed," Bill-E chuckles. It's the morning after. We're on our way to class.

"I don't want to talk about it," I mutter.

"I just don't see how you could —"

"Enough!" I snap. Then, softly, "Remember what I told you about my parents? How they died?"

"Oh. Yeah." Bill-E's face drops. "Grubbs, I didn't mean —"

"It's OK. Just don't say anything about it. Please? To the others?"

"Of course not," Bill-E smiles. "This stays between us. I'll never breathe a word of it to anyone, especially not Bo Kooniart and her gang. They'd have to torture it out of me."

"Thanks. Because, if they knew . . ."

"Like I said, your secret's safe with me," Bill-E promises. "Dervish won't say anything either, or Juni. Nobody will ever find out. It'll be coolio."

✠ "Look out!" Bo screams as we walk into class. "It's a demon!"

Bo, Abe, Vanalee, Salit — even Kuk and Kik — howl theatrically, then burst out laughing. Miss Jaun blinks at them, astonished. I groan and raise my eyebrows at Bill-E, who can only shrug, bewildered.

"My dad was in the hall outside your room," Bo says smugly. "He heard you talking. He heard *everything*." She laughs again, and I know I'm in for a *long* few months.

MISSING

✠　　✠　　✠

THE joke doesn't wear thin for Bo. Every day she drags it out, mocking and ridiculing me, keeping the story of my hysterics alive. She tells anyone who'll listen, the other actors, the crew, Davida. Most smile and dismiss it, too busy to bother about such trivial matters. But knowing they know causes me to blush fiercely every time somebody even glances at me sideways.

Emmet never called back and I'm too shamefaced to call him. I doubt if he'll have heard about my panic attack, but there's no telling how far Bo might have decided to spread the joke.

The person I'm angriest with — other than myself, for being such an idiot — is Tump Kooniart. I can't blame Bo for wringing such wicked pleasure out of my embarrassment — it would be hard for any kid to ignore such a juicy bit of bait if it fell into their lap. But why was her father sneaking around outside our room? And why didn't he keep his big mouth shut? If Dervish had heard something like this about Bo, he wouldn't have told me. Tump Kooniart should have kept quiet. He didn't. So now it's payback time!

✠ I spend a lot of hours thinking about ways to get even with Bo's father. Itching powder in his clothes? Rat droppings in his soup? Human droppings in his stew or chocolate ice cream?!? Shave him bald or glue his lips together while he sleeps?

All good stuff, but basic. I want something that'll give him a scare, that I can use to humiliate him. Like, if he's scared of rats, borrow one of the trained rats that are being used in the film, drop it down the back of his shirt when there's a crowd around, laugh my head off as he writhes and screams. But to do that, I'll have to find out more about him and what he's scared of.

So I start shadowing him. I do it when I'm not in class. I don't tell Bill-E. He'd happily join in if he knew what I was up to, but I don't want him getting into trouble if this back-fires. Tump Kooniart's a powerful player. If I humble him in public, I might end up being booted off the set. I don't mind that, but there's no need for Bill-E to suffer too.

Tump's easy to follow. Tall and wide, always dressed in a drab brown suit. He walks with a slow waddle, mopping sweat from his forehead with a handkerchief that rarely leaves his hand. He usually talks loudly as he strolls, to himself if no one's with him. He doesn't seem to be able to keep silent, except when a scene is being filmed. I bet he even talks in his sleep. If I was blind, I could probably follow him by sound alone.

I don't learn much about Tump, except he loves to talk

and eat. He has a trailer on the western edge of Slawter, separate trailers beside it for Bo and Abe. Three of the biggest trailers on the set. When he's not on the prowl, making sure his actors are happy, or pigging out in one of the cafeterias, he spends most of his time in the trailer. He makes lots of phone calls. There are no personal computers allowed in Slawter — no video mobiles either — so he has to work a huge Filofax in which he keeps all his contact details and other info. I think about stealing the Filofax and burning it, but that's hardly going to leave him a trembling wreck!

✜ Close to Tump's trailer, nearly a week after I began shadowing him. Waiting for him to emerge, sitting in the shade of another trailer, reading a movie magazine — always plenty of those around. Starting to tire of the detective work. Bo's still annoying me, but her insults have grown stale. Nobody really laughs at her jokes anymore. Maybe I should quit this game and forget about vengeance.

Someone knocks on Tump's door. I look up and spot Chuda Sool entering the trailer. I haven't spoken to Chuda since the day of the "demon" attack. I'm sure Bo has told him about my hysterics. He must think I'm a real nutjob. He might even feel insulted that I didn't believe him when he told me about Nora and Tump.

"Look what the cat dragged in," someone says behind me. I jump, but it's only Bo, on her way back from filming. "Discover any demons today, Grady?"

"No. Discover any new jokes?"

"Don't need them. Not when the old ones are still funny." She flashes her teeth and growls demonically. I yawn and focus on my magazine until she loses interest and goes away. I wait for the sound of her trailer door locking, then get up, angry, sick of hanging around. I could be playing foosball with Bill-E, not sitting here like a third-rate substitute, wasting my —

Tump steps out of his trailer, followed by Chuda Sool. Tump's talking loudly, mopping away busily at his forehead. Chuda never seems to sweat, which is handy — without eyebrows, sweat would flow straight into his eyes. The pair set off in a northerly direction, looking a bit like Laurel and Hardy from the rear. Since I'm here, I decide to follow. But this is the last time. I've had enough.

Tump and Chuda head for the D workshops. The huge warehouse dominates the northern part of Slawter. I haven't spent much time up here — no point, since access to the workshops is strictly prohibited. As Tump and Chuda show their passes to a security guard on the western door — one of four doors leading into the warehouse — I hang back and take a long look at the building.

Three storeys high, two hundred and fifty feet wide, maybe four hundred feet long. Large, unplastered block walls. A flat roof. No windows. Grey and featureless, apart from a big red D painted on the wall above the door. A small guard's hut to the right of the entrance.

I'd love to have a look inside, at the monster costumes and puppets. A small part of me still believes the demon was real. If I could check out the costumes, perhaps it would help convince me of the truth. But hardly anyone is allowed to enter the hallowed halls of the D workshops. Even Dervish has only seen a small section of the complex.

I wait impatiently for Tump and Chuda to come out. Then I figure, screw them! I'm through with this crap. I decide to find Bill-E and hang out with him for the rest of the afternoon. But before leaving, I wander around the warehouse, on the off chance that one of the doors is open, its guard asleep in his hut. That won't happen, of course, but I might as well give it a shot while I'm here.

The guard on the southern door studies me suspiciously as I approach. Though he doesn't openly carry any weapons, it wouldn't surprise me if he had a gun hidden on him somewhere. I smile politely and don't stray any closer. Walk to the eastern end and turn left. The door on this side is shut too, and although the guard's in his hut, he isn't asleep — I spot him through the window as I walk past, leafing through a magazine with pictures of tanks on the cover.

I reach the northern end and turn left again. The guard here is standing next to the door, leaning against the wall. He smiles as I go past. I think about stopping to chat, maybe try to smooth talk my way inside, but his smile isn't *that* inviting.

Back to the western end again. Heading south, thinking about where Bill-E might be. As I come up to the guard's hut, the door to the workshops opens. I hear Tump's voice and stop behind the hut, where he and Chuda can't see me, to wait until they pass.

". . . not going to like it," Tump is booming.

"They're not supposed to like it," Chuda replies, in a much softer voice.

"But the boy will be hard to keep quiet. They're so close to each other. Maybe we should take them both."

"One will be enough," Chuda says. "Now all we have to . . ."

Their voices fade. I remain where I am, frowning, wondering who and what they were talking about.

✠ The next day, Kik is missing.

Kuk turns up for class by himself, looking lost. "Have any of you seen Kik?" he asks, eyes darting around the room as if his twin sister might be hiding behind a desk. "I can't find her. I don't know where she is. Kik? Are you here?"

Miss Jaun sits the agitated Kuk down, tries to soothe his nerves, and coaxes the story out of him. It's not complicated. He awoke this morning and Kik's bed was empty. He couldn't find her. Their dad wasn't too concerned — said she'd probably gone for a walk — but Kuk smelled a rat immediately.

"We don't go anywhere without telling each other. She wouldn't have slipped out without saying anything."

"Maybe she just needed to be alone for a while," Miss Jaun suggests.

"We don't like being alone," Kuk says, shaking his head vigorously. "Alone is bad. Alone is scary."

When Miss Jaun fails to calm Kuk's nerves, she calls security and asks a guard if he can put the word out to look for Kik. "It's no big deal," she tells him. "We'd just like to know where she is."

Class proceeds as normal, except for Kuk, who fidgets behind his desk, eyes wide and searching, staring out the window. He unnerves the rest of us. Even Bo is discomfited by him and remains quiet, no jokes or digs.

Towards the end of class, Miss Jaun summons the guard again. He says nobody has seen Kik but they're still looking.

I raise a hand. "Have you tried the D workshops?" I ask innocently.

The guard frowns. "She wouldn't be there."

"She might have snuck in."

The guard grins. "Into the D? I don't think so. Even I haven't been inside — I don't have clearance."

"But she *might* be there," I insist. I'm holding a steel ball-point pen, gripping it tight, remembering the conversation I overheard yesterday, Tump saying that "the boy will be hard to keep quiet."

"I'll check with the guys who were on duty this morning," the guard says, rolling his eyes slightly. "If they've seen her, I'll let you know."

"Thanks."

The guard leaves. Class ends. Kuk hurries out to search for his sister.

"What was that about the D warehouse?" Bill-E asks, hanging back.

"Nothing. I just thought they might not have looked there."

Bill-E squints suspiciously. "I know you too well, Grubbs Grady," he says in a bad Bela Lugosi accent. "You wouldn't have said something like that without a reason. What are you hiding from me?"

I consider telling him what I heard Tump Kooniart say. But I'm still smarting from my previous humiliation. I don't want to reveal my fears, only for Kik to turn up, leaving me looking like a paranoid maniac.

"It's nothing," I say, unclenching my fist to lay my pen down. "Let's . . ."

Grey liquid drips from my hands onto the table. Bill-E pulls a face. "What's that?" he asks. "It looks like mercury."

I don't reply. I'm staring at the liquid, the last few drops dripping from my fingers, black ink bubbling on my palms. It's the remains of the pen. The steel ballpoint I was holding.

I melted it.

✠ Night falls. Kik hasn't been seen all day. Kuk's not the only one worried about her now. Her father's frantic. The search has intensified. The security forces have been deployed in earnest. Davida even suspended shooting so everyone could the search parties and help.

I'm with a group exploring the eastern end of town, going through all the real buildings, checking behind the façades of the fakes. Trying to focus on the search. Trying not to think about the pen and how I melted it. But I can't *not* think about it. There *could* be a scientific explanation. But I'm certain the melting had nothing to do with science. It was *magic*.

I'm not a natural magician. Dervish told me that only one or two real magicians are born every century. There are others like Dervish and Meera Flame — mages — with the potential to perform acts of magic, usually with the aid of spells. I could maybe do that. But I never have. I don't care for magic. Plus, there hasn't been time. Dervish was a zombie for more than a year, and hasn't been up for teaching duties since he recovered.

So how did I melt the pen?

There's only one answer I can think of. When demons

enter our universe, they affect the area where they cross. They're creatures of magic, and that magic infects the world around them. When my parents were killed, I was able to tap into the magical, demonic energy and use it to escape. I did it again, later, in the secret cellar, when I fought Artery and Vein.

I think that's happening now. There's magic in the air — the magic of demons.

✠ We don't find Kik. The search concludes after midnight. Everybody turns in. Most people reckon she ran away. The guards say they'll search for her beyond Slawter tomorrow, take Kuk and his father with them.

I haven't told anyone about my fears. No point — I'd only be laughed at. But I can't sit back and do nothing. I have to try to help Kik, assuming she *can* still be helped. So I track down Dervish. He's been searching with Juni and a few others. He and Juni aren't an item yet, but they've been spending more and more time together, and she's with him now. He says she's helping him cope with his nightmares, that she's taught him how to control his dreams, to keep the monsters of his subconscious at bay. But I think he's more lustful than grateful — he's practically bathing in that new aftershave now!

I get my story straight before I hit Dervish with it. I say I saw Kik yesterday, near the D workshops. Tell him I think she found a way in, that she's hiding inside, possibly trapped. "Maybe something fell on her. She could be pinned to the floor, crying out for help, nobody around to hear."

Dervish doesn't think she could get in — security's too

tight. But Juni says they should check it out. "Grubbs is right. It's the one place we haven't explored. If she did somehow sneak in, and had an accident . . ."

Neither Juni nor Dervish has the authority to enter the D workshops, so we go to Davida. We find her in her office, discussing the next day's shoot with Chuda Sool. Davida's tired and irritable — the delay has put her a day behind schedule. She hears us out, then shakes her head. "We already checked. Grubbs mentioned the D earlier, so the guards who were on duty this morning — and last night — were questioned. They all said they hadn't seen her."

"But they wouldn't have if she snuck in," Dervish presses.

"Impossible," Chuda says and I catch him shooting a glare at me. "There are no ways into the D warehouse other than through the doors. We constructed it to be impenetrable."

"But —" Dervish begins.

"No," Chuda snaps, staring at Dervish directly.

Dervish stares back at Chuda, his pupils widening. Then he smiles and shrugs. "Guess we were wrong."

Chuda nods, his eyes still fixed on Dervish. "I guess you were."

My stomach tenses. It's not like Dervish to back down so easily. Is Chuda controlling Dervish's thoughts? Was I right about the browless assistant director? Is he in league with demonic forces?

Before I can challenge Chuda, Juni speaks up. "We need to search there," she tells Davida. "Or, if you won't allow us in, send in a team of guards and tell them to search the place with a fine-tooth comb. Because if Kik is in there — and a determined child can always find a way in, no matter how tight the security — she might be in trouble. If we ignore that, and something bad happens to her . . ."

Davida sighs. "Chuda, assemble a team of guards and —"

"I think you should oversee this personally, Davida," Juni interrupts. She smiles sweetly at the glowering Chuda. "No offense, Mr. Sool, but you're too convinced the girl isn't there. You might just take a cursory glance around, then quit."

Chuda bristles angrily and squares up to Juni. Before he can speak, Davida says, "We'll have no infighting, thank you. Chuda, please assemble a team for me. I'll go with them into the D workshops and make sure every room and cupboard is scoured methodically. Is that acceptable, Miss Swan?"

"Perfect," Juni smiles and we file out. I walk just behind Dervish, studying him carefully, worried about what might be going on inside his head.

✠ We wait outside the warehouse while Davida and the guards search for Kik. Juni is concerned about Dervish. She asks if he feels all right, if he has a headache. She saw it too, the exchange between him and Chuda. I doubt if she understood it the way I did, but she knows — or senses — something isn't right.

It's after two-thirty in the morning when a yawning Davida and her guards emerge. She shakes her head, exasperated. "No sign of the girl. We checked everywhere."

"You're sure?" I ask.

Davida doesn't answer. "We'll search around the

countryside tomorrow," she tells Juni. "The girl probably had an argument with one of the other children and took off in a huff. Maybe she'll turn up by herself."

I smother a snort and mutter, "I doubt it!"

✠ I set the alarm an hour later and sleep in. Stare at the ceiling when I wake, tired and grumpy, finding it hard to get out of bed. Wondering what to do about Kik. Ideally I'd like to tell Dervish what I heard Tump Kooniart and Chuda Sool saying. Insist that Emmet *was* butchered by a demon, and Kik . . .

But I spoke to Emmet. He wasn't killed. Unless . . .

You can do just about anything with movie technology or magic. Maybe Chuda Sool was eavesdropping with Tump Kooniart when I told Dervish and Juni my fears. Perhaps he intercepted the call and faked Emmet's voice, using either a mechanical or magical vocal distorter. Difficult — but not impossible.

I grab my pants from the chair at the foot of my bed, dig my cell out of its pocket, and dial Emmet's number. There's no ringing at his end. His phone's turned off, or he's somewhere without a signal.

I get up, dress, and head for class. I think about asking Juni for alternate phone numbers for Emmet and his mom, but she'd probably want to know why I was looking for them now. I don't want to reveal my suspicions to anyone in case I end up a laughingstock again. So, at the end of class, I casually ask Miss Jaun if she has Mrs. Eijit's number. I say I've been trying to contact Emmet on his cell but haven't been able to get through. Miss Jaun searches her list of names, then calls the number out to me. I thank her and dial it as I head for lunch. Dead, like Emmet's. I try his number again — the same as earlier.

It might not mean anything. Then again, it might.

✠ I try the two numbers several times over the course of the day. Not a peep out of either. I dial information and get their home number. Call it, only to find that the line has been disconnected.

One last try. I remember Emmet telling us about his local school. Again I use information, then call and ask if I can speak with Emmet Eijit. I say I found his cell phone and want to return it. The secretary says Emmet's not at school, he's making a film. I say I thought he'd finished and returned. No, she says, he hasn't. I ask if she's sure, if maybe he's back home, just not at school. She says definitely not, she knows his mother.

I stare at my phone a long time after that, certain I've been tricked. Emmet and his mom are still here, along with Kik — but not necessarily alive.

✠ Night. Kik hasn't been found. The search teams return at seven. Kuk and his father aren't with them. The searchers say Mr. Kane and his son have gone home, in case Kik heads there. I groan when I hear that. I hope it's true. I pray that it is. Not just because I don't want Kuk and his dad to be dead — but because if it's a lie, it means the guards who were with them are part of a cover-up. It means it isn't just Chuda Sool and one or two others I have to be wary of. I might not be able to trust anybody in the entire cast and crew.

✠ Filming resumes in the morning. Davida's still worried about the missing Kik (or claims to be — *who can I trust?*), but life must go on. A film costs a fortune to make. Every day is vital. She can't afford to have her team sitting around idle. So, while a selection of guards takes off to search the lands around Slawter as the sun rises, the cameras roll as normal.

They're filming the second big demon scene tonight. No carnage or loss of life this time. It's a scene from the third act, in which a demon appears to Bobby Mint and his friends. It predicts doom, warns them of the destruction to come, then tells them they can't leave, it's too late, they're destined to die, along with everyone they care about and love.

I've lost interest in filming but I have to go watch tonight's shoot, to check out the demon. I've heard it's different from the one that killed Emmet. I wonder if this creature will be real or a model? I know what I'd put my money on!

✠ A large crowd gathers for the shoot, but not as many as at the first demon show. This scene's being shot outside a church, one of the fake buildings in Slawter. In the script, the heroes have gathered inside to discuss the demons and what they can do to alert others to the danger. Those scenes have been filmed — or will be — on an interior set. This scene is set at the end of their debate. They've just come out. As they're heading down the steps, the demon appears out of the church behind them, laughing, saying it's over-heard their entire plan.

Davida sets the scene, runs the actors through their paces, makes sure all the cameras and lights are correctly positioned, then takes her seat. Action!

I watch nervously, holding my breath, as Salit Smit and the others spill out of the church, faces bright and determined. There are eight steps down from the doors. As they hit the second from bottom step, laughter echoes from within.

"Poor, foolish humans," the demon crows. Salit and his crew whirl, gasping. "You think you know so much. But, like all mortals, your knowledge of the world is pitiful. It would be amusing, were it not so sad."

I start to shiver at the first syllable. There's no mistaking that voice, the low, mournful tone. I know what's coming next. I'd give anything to be wrong but I know I'm not.

The demon appears, gliding out of the shadows. He's lit perfectly. I hear murmurs of approval from the people around me. They were caught by surprise with Emmet, but they're ready this time, in control of their emotions. Besides, although this demon is more horrific in appearance than the first, he moves so fluidly and gracefully that they have time to appreciate his design, the months of hard work that must have gone into creating him.

"You cannot defeat me or my kind," the demon says, looking from one so-called hero to another, then beyond, to the crowd watching the filming. "We can go anywhere you can, and to places where you can't. We see all, hear all, know all. And we will *kill* all."

A tall demon, pale red skin with lots of cracks in it, from which blood continually oozes. Dark red eyes. No hair or nose. Grey teeth and tongue. A hole where his heart should be, filled with dozens of tiny snakes. Mangled hands at the ends of eight arms. No feet, just fleshy strips dangling from his waist, giving the appearance of thin, misshapen legs. He doesn't touch the floor, but hovers a few inches above the ground all the time.

"This is our town now, or soon will be," the demon says. "There is nothing you can do to stop us." His eyes fall on me and he smiles widely. "There is nothing *any* of you can do — except be *slaughtered.*"

Then he laughs and drifts back into the church. The doors slam shut. A boy in the group of heroes screams. Davida yells, "Cut!"

Everyone pours forward, cheering, congratulating the actors, remarking on how realistic and creepy the demon was, questioning how the effects team got it to hover so believably, what mechanics were involved.

But there were no strings or engines. It wasn't a model or costume. The few doubts I had up to this point vanish. We're in seriously deep trouble. The demon wasn't speaking from a script. His words weren't meant for the fictional characters — but for those of us watching.

There *are* real demons here. Emmet *has* been killed, and probably Kik and her relatives too. And it's going to get worse. Because the monster who wowed the crowd a minute ago is the one who killed my parents and sister, who vowed to kill Dervish, Bill-E, and me . . . the majestic, terrible demon master himself . . . lowly *Lord Loss.*

D

✠   ✠   ✠

INCREDIBLY, impossibly, Dervish doesn't believe me.

"It was just another guy in a costume," he says. "You have to stop seeing demons everywhere you look. I know —"

"Don't!" I snap. I've gotten him by himself, out of earshot of everybody. "That piece of scum killed my mom and dad. He slaughtered Gret. Don't tell me I could ever confuse a movie prop for the real thing. Don't you dare."

"Grubbs, I know this is hard, but you've got to believe —"

"That was Lord Loss!" I cry.

"It looked like him," Dervish says soothingly, "but that's because Davida did a lot of research. She knows what real demons look like. Actually, I helped her out on this one. She had some of the details wrong. She didn't know about the cracks in his skin, the color of his eyes, or that he didn't have real feet."

"Really?" I sneer. "And you filled her in on the facts?"

"Yes," Dervish says, trying to sound modest.

"And her technicians were able to make the changes" —
I snap my fingers — "*like that*? They were able to take
elaborate, mechanized costumes they'd been working on for
months and alter them within the space of a few days?"

"Yes," Dervish says evenly.

I stare into my uncle's eyes but I don't find him there. The
Dervish I know wouldn't smile at me glibly like this and dis-
miss my fears so carelessly. Chuda Sool has brainwashed
him, I'm sure of it. I'll have to look elsewhere for allies.

"Where are you going?" Dervish asks as I turn my back on
him and march off.

"To find someone who'll believe."

✠ I ask Juni to visit Bill-E and me in our room. I say it's
about Bo Kooniart, that I'm having problems with her and
would like Juni's advice. Naturally, Juni's only too happy to
help. Promises to drop by within the next half hour.

Bill-E knows something big is up. He doesn't know what
it is, but he's delighted to be involved, proud that I'm in-
cluding him. He wasn't happy when I skulked around the set
without him, not saying why, but now that I'm bringing him
in on the secret, all is forgiven.

I say nothing until Juni arrives, getting things clear in my
head, deciding how much to tell them, what to say and what
to keep to myself. When she's finally here, sitting on a chair,
hands clasped on her knees, I begin by confessing that I lied.
"I didn't really bring you here to talk about Bo."

"I guessed," she smiles. "You're not a good liar. Which is a
positive thing — don't think I'm criticizing you!"

"Before I get down to the crazy stuff, have either of you noticed anything strange about Dervish?" I ask.

"What do you mean?" Bill-E frowns.

"I'll take that as a no. Juni?"

She pauses. "I don't know your uncle very well, but he's seemed a little . . . unfocused recently."

"You saw it when he was talking with Chuda about the search for Kik, didn't you?"

"I saw . . . something," Juni says cagily. "Dervish has been through a lot these last two years. The responsibility of having to look after you, the temporary loss of his mind, trying to readjust to normal life, the nightmares."

"Nightmares?" Bill-E asks. We never told him about Dervish's bad dreams.

"He's had trouble sleeping recently," Juni explains.

"That's the first I've heard of it," Bill-E grumbles.

"He finds it easy to share his secrets and fears with me," Juni says. "He's able to tell me things he finds hard to discuss with others. I've been trying to help him sort through his problems. We were making good progress but now he seems to have regressed."

"Chuda's messing with his mind," I tell her, "controlling his thoughts."

"You can't be serious," Juni laughs. But her laughter dies away when she sees that I am.

"I'm going to tell you something that will sound insane," I begin. "Bill-E knows some of it but not all. I need you to hear me out and at least try to believe me."

"Of course," Juni says, leaning forward, intrigued.

I take a deep breath. Glance at Bill-E, knowing what I say is going to hurt him, then launch straight in. "Demons killed my parents and sister . . ."

✠ I fill them in on most of the details. My early encounter with Lord Loss. Escape. Madness. Recovery. Moving to Carcery Vale. The curse of the Gradys. Then the big one — Bill-E turning into a werewolf.

"So that's it!" Bill-E cries. He's trembling, his lazy eyelid quivering wildly. "I never bought your story that Dervish locked me up to protect me. I knew there was something you weren't telling." He glares at me accusingly. "You lied to me."

"We didn't want to hurt you," I sigh.

"I can take hurt. Not lies. You should have told me."

"Maybe," I mutter miserably.

"So, am I cured?" Bill-E snarls.

"Yes."

"For real? For ever?"

I nod glumly, then outline the deal certain members of our family had going with Lord Loss, the chess matches, the battles with his familiars. I tell them how Dervish and I challenged Lord Loss on Bill-E's behalf. The only part I leave out is the truth about Bill-E's father. I don't tell him we had the same dad. This isn't the time to open that can of worms.

Bill-E's rage dwindles away as he hears what Dervish and I risked to save him. He's staring at me with awe now, tears trickling down his cheeks. I find that more unsettling than his anger. He's gawking at me as if I'm some kind of hero. But I'm not. I only did it because he's my brother, but I can't tell him that, not now. He thinks Dervish is his dad. If I told him the truth, I'd be hitting him with the news that his real father's dead.

I finish quickly with the last few months, Dervish defeating Lord Loss in his demonic realm and regaining his senses, the nightmares, coming here to try and sort himself out, the demon that killed Emmet, overhearing Tump Kooniart and Chuda Sool talking, the appearance of Lord Loss.

"It was definitely him," I tell them. "I wasn't a hundred percent sure before, but now I am. There are real demons in Slawter. Chuda and Tump are working for them, along with some of the crew. Davida might be one of their allies, too. Others as well. Lord Loss swore revenge on me, Dervish, and Bill-E. So the three of us are for the chop, no doubt about it. Probably the rest of you as well."

Silence. Bill-E is staring at me, torn between hero worship, terror, and doubt. Juni doesn't know what to think or say. She's probably heard all sorts in her time, but nothing like this. She's trying to think of a gentle way of denying what I'm saying, without insulting or enraging me.

"It's OK," I smile. "You can say I'm crazy. I won't mind."

"People roll out that word too swiftly," Juni objects. "It's an easy fall-back. I try never to make such gross generalizations. But . . ."

". . . in this case you'll make an exception," I finish for her.

She grins shakily. "I wasn't going to say that."

"But you were thinking it, right?"

She tilts her head uncertainly. "We have a lot to discuss. This goes back a long way. You have deep-rooted issues we'll have to work through, one at a time. To begin with —"

"Do you believe in magic?" I interrupt.

"No," Juni says plainly.

"What if I could convince you?"

"How?"

I've been thinking a lot about this. I knew words alone wouldn't be enough. I haven't done anything magical since melting the pen, but I'm sure magic is still in the air, surrounding me, waiting to be channeled. It had better be, or else I really will look like a loon!

"Is that worth a lot?" I ask, pointing at the watch on her wrist.

"No," she frowns.

"Does it matter to you? Would you miss it if you lost it?"

"Not really. Where is this going, Grubbs?"

"You'll see." I fix my gaze on the watch, willing it to melt. I'm anticipating a struggle, but almost as soon as I focus, the watch liquefies and drips off Juni's hand.

"Ow!" Juni yelps, leaping to her feet and rubbing her wrist. "It's hot!"

"Sorry!" I jump up too. "Are you OK? Do you want me to get some ice or —"

"I'm fine," Juni snaps, then quits rubbing, stares at the red mark left behind by the melted metal, then at the puddle on the floor, then at me. "Grubbs . . . what the hell?" she croaks.

"That was just for openers," I beam, confidence bubbling up. "Have you ever wanted to fly?"

✠ In the end we don't fly. Juni isn't ready to open the window and soar over the buildings of Slawter. I'm not either, really. But we levitate a bit, to prove that the melting watch wasn't a hoax, that this is real magic, not some stage trick.

"This is incredible!" Juni laughs as I make the light switch on and off just by looking at it, while juggling six pairs of balled-up socks without touching them.

"Totally amazing is what it is!" Bill-E gasps. "Could I do that too?"

"Maybe," I say, flicking the light on and off a few more times, then letting the socks drop. "Dervish said lots of people have magical potential. They just don't know it. The magic's thick in the air around us here, but you and the others aren't aware of it. I am, because I fought demons and part of my mind — the part that's magic — opened up. If you could open that part of *your* mind, I bet you could do everything I can."

"I need to get me a demon to whup," Bill-E mutters.

"Of course, it could all be in my head," Juni says. "You could have slipped me hallucinogenic substances. I might be imagining the watch, floating, the socks."

Bill-E wrinkles his nose. "You couldn't hallucinate the smell of Grubbs's socks!" he says and we all laugh.

"You don't really believe that, do you?" I ask Juni.

"No," she sighs. "But I want to keep an open mind, like you advised. That means not accepting your story about demons even if the magic is real." She looks at me earnestly. "One doesn't verify the other. I haven't seen any evidence of demons yet."

"You don't need to!" I groan. "If demons aren't real, where am I getting my power from?"

"I have no idea," Juni says. "You might be generating it naturally, subconsciously. The demons might simply be your way of rationalizing your powers." She holds up a hand as I start to argue. "I'm not saying that *is* the case — just that it *might* be."

Juni sits back, a troubled look on her face. "Actually, I can't tell you how much I hope that the demons *are* a product of your imagination. For Emmet's sake, Kik's, and the others."

"I know," I mutter. "I wish they weren't real too. But they are."

She licks her lips, frowning deeply, trying to get a handle on what I'm telling her. "I need proof," she finally says. "I'm not sure what you want me to do, but I can't do anything until I've seen direct evidence."

"I want you to help Dervish," I tell her. "Chuda Sool has some sort mind lock on him. I want you to help me break it. You can do that without believing in demons, can't you?"

"Perhaps," she says. "But I don't want to go anywhere near your uncle's mind until I know for sure what I'm dealing with."

"I think I *can* prove it," I say softly, lowering my gaze. "But it could be dangerous. The sort of dangerous where we all die horribly if things go wrong."

"I'm prepared to take that risk," Juni says evenly.

"Me too," Bill-E pipes up bravely, though the squeak in his voice betrays his fear.

I nod reluctantly. "Demons don't appear out of thin air. They have to be summoned. Their universe has to merge with ours. A window or tunnel between worlds has to be opened. If Lord Loss and the other demon were real, there has to be a place where they crossed. A secret place. A place nobody but their human partners can get into."

"The D workshops," Bill-E and Juni say at the exact same time.

"Got it in one," I chuckle bleakly.

✠ Juni keeps saying she must be crazy for going along with this, it's a mad plan, she should have her head examined. But the magic unnerved her. She's confused, not in complete control. I should give her a day to think things over and clear her head. But she might not play ball if I did. She might start rationalizing and analyzing, and decide nobody in her position should break into a building. Worse — she might tell Davida what I believe and tip our enemies off. So I rush her along, allowing her no time to think.

It's impossible to sneak up on the D warehouse, no matter what time you come. Large, powerful lights are trained on all sides of the building at night. You can't approach it without your shadow preceding you, growing like a giant's the closer you get.

But I've got magic on my side. I could have performed any number of miracles in our room to convince Juni of my power. I didn't randomly choose to experiment on the lightbulb.

Studying the lights from the shelter of the closest building to the warehouse. Juni and Bill-E are quiet behind me. I can't see all the lights from here, but I can imagine them.

Not sure if I have the strength to do this. Just have to try and hope for the best. Focusing, I close my eyes, keeping the picture of the lights vivid in my thoughts. I visualize the lights flaring and going out, all at once, like a flashbulb on a camera. Call on the magic. Try to extend it to the lights. Doubting if I can really —

Bill-E gasps. Then a chuckle. "Coolio!"

I open my eyes to darkness. "Let's go," I hiss, starting forward, not sure how much time we'll have.

"Oh my," Juni says breathlessly. But she runs after me with Bill-E, along for the ride even if she doesn't truly want to be.

✠ The guards come out of their hut with strong flashlights. We drop to our stomachs as their beams sweep the surrounding area. I think about quenching the flashlights, but that would really stir up their suspicions.

Lying on the cool ground, head down. I hear one of the guards on his walkie-talkie, checking if the lights are out all over. He doesn't sound worried. The guards sweep the area a few more times with their flashlights, then return to the hut. One keeps his flashlight trained on the door of the D. There's no way we could get in through it without being seen. So it's just as well that I didn't plan on entering that way.

Rising, I hurry forward, trying not to make any noise, heading for a point about three-quarters of the way along the side of the warehouse, where it's nice and dark, where we can't be easily seen by the guards.

I rest when I get to the wall, panting heavily, more from fear than the run. Juni and Bill-E arrive moments later. Bill-E's puffing hard — he's not as in shape as me. I can see their faces in the light of the moon and stars. Bill-E looks scared but excited. Juni's just scared. Funny, but I feel like the adult here.

"What now?" Bill-E asks when he gets his breath back.

"The Indian rope trick," I grin, then try to make a length

of rope appear, dangling from the roof. Nothing happens. I try again, this time demanding the rope to simply appear on the ground. Nothing.

I frown, wondering if I used up all my magic quenching the lights. But then I recall my fight with Artery and Vein. Dervish supplied the weapons, laid them on the floor of the secret cellar, axes, swords, and so on. He wouldn't have gone to all that effort if we could have simply made weapons appear. Maybe magic doesn't work that way and objects can't be created out of thin air.

So the roof's out. Fine. Time for Plan B.

I focus on the wall. Bare blocks, cemented tightly together. No chinks. Can't tell how thick they are, but I imagine the wall's more than a single block deep. I place my left hand on the nearest block and concentrate. Not sure if I can melt stone like metal, but I give it a go.

The block doesn't melt. I try again but still it holds. I sigh — looks like I've run out of ideas. But as I lean forward, trying to think of some other way in, my fingers gouge into the stone. It's like putting my hand in mud. I make a half-fist and scoop out a handful of mushy material. I smile at the muck, then at Juni and Bill-E. "You two clear the mess away," I tell them. "I'll get to work on the rest of the blocks."

"Be careful," Bill-E whispers. "We don't want the wall collapsing."

"No worries," I snort. "Grubbs Grady's on top of the situation!"

"This is madness," Juni mutters, but digs her fingers into the semi-melted block and begins scooping it out.

✠ It takes fifteen minutes to gouge a hole big enough for us to fit through. It feels like hours. All the time I'm aware of the threat of the lights snapping back on, the guards sighting us, everything coming undone.

But the darkness holds and at last I melt through the third and final layer of blocks. I poke my head through the gap and switch on the flashlight I brought with me. This looks like an ordinary props room — puppets and molds lying around, tools, mannequins, bits of material, tubes of glue. I switch off the flashlight and slide forward. Juni follows, then Bill-E.

Bill-E's frowning when he steps in. He looks back at the hole. "What are we going to do about that?" he asks. "If they see it when the lights come on . . ."

"We just have to hope they don't."

"And when we leave?" he persists. "They'll know we've been here."

"I'll try to make the stones solid again and put them back," I tell him. "But if I can't, don't worry. If I'm right, and we're dealing with demons, we're not going to hang around like horror movie victims, waiting for them to get wise to us."

"And if you're wrong?" Juni asks. "If there aren't any demons?"

"Then we'll wind up in a heap of trouble," I chuckle. "But it'll be trouble of the butt-kicking, job-losing kind, and trouble like that I don't mind so much."

"So what now?" Bill-E asks, glancing around.

"We wander. Explore as much of the building as we can.

Keep going until we find something strange or run out of rooms."

"Perhaps one of us should remain here, to alert the others if the guards find the hole," Bill-E suggests.

"How?" I grunt.

"Phone." He roots out his mobile, flicks it on, frowns, shakes it, then scowls. "No signal. Damn."

"It's probably better if we stay together anyway," Juni says, then lets out an uneasy breath. "I've never done anything like this. I never even stole candy from a store when I was a child. I've always respected the law."

"Welcome to the underworld, baby!" Bill-E chortles, trying to sound like a 1930s gangster.

"No more talking," I whisper.

We advance.

FRESH MEAT

✠   ✠   ✠

WE don't spot any security cameras. I guess Chuda Sool or his superiors thought the armed guards outside would provide enough protection. Or there are hidden cameras we can't see. Or they didn't think anyone who found their way in would be able to get out.

Winding through the building, one ordinary room giving way to another. Lots of weird, demon-shaped puppets on display, but the work of human hands. Cleverly constructed, but hardly hewn in the fires of hell. Plastic, metal, rubber — not flesh, bone, blood.

I try not to lose confidence as we push further into the warehouse. It's logical that they'd have an outer ring of genuine workshops. While this place is off-limits, some of the crew — like Dervish — have been allowed into parts of it. This is camouflage. Things will be different further in.

I hope.

I fear.

✠ We come to a massive steel door unlike any of the others we've encountered. The full height of the ceiling and ten feet wide. There's a small digital screen on the right-hand side, the outline of a hand printed on it.

"Fingerprint controlled," Bill-E notes, rapping the door with his knuckles. He reaches out to press his hand on the screen.

"Wait," I stop him. "It might sound an alarm if an intruder touches it."

Bill-E lowers his hand. "We gonna melt our way through the wall, boss?"

"Reckon so, kemosabe."

I lay my fingers on the blocks to the right of the door. Focus my magic and tell the stone to melt. Push forward to scoop out the first handful of molten rock.

It's solid.

I try again — no luck. Rubbing my fingers together, trying to figure it out. It can't be that I'm running low on juice — there's more magic in the air here than outside. I can feel it practically crackling around me. Just to be sure, I make myself rise a foot and a half off the ground. No problem.

"Something wrong?" Juni asks, eyeing me nervously as I float in the air.

"The wall's protected," I tell her, smoothly descending. "It's been charged with magic, or there's magic pushing out from within. I can't melt it."

"We could try somewhere else," Bill-E says. "There might be another door or a part of the wall that isn't . . ."

I shake my head. "It's going to be like this all the way round. I can sense it — literally. There's an inner structure, a building within the warehouse. If there are other doors, they'll be like this. The wall will be the same everywhere too. And the roof."

"Then we can't go on," Juni notes with relief. "Let's get out, plug up the hole we made, and discuss a new —"

"No," I cut her short. "I'm not stopping. Not until I've convinced you."

"But if we can't get through . . ." she protests gently.

"I didn't say that. We just have to be a bit smarter."

I move back to the screen and study the outline of the hand. My magic's not strong enough to combat the magic of the wall, but maybe I can outfox the technology of the door.

I place my right hand on the screen, tensing in case alarms sound. But there's no noisy alarm. Lights don't flash. Breathing softly, thinking hard, trying to direct magic into the screen. It's set up to recognize certain fingerprints. I want to tell it that my prints are among those it accepts. But how do you talk to a computer that only understands binary code?

I ignore the complications. Send a simple message, over and over, letting magic flow all the time. "You know me. My prints are in your database. *Open.*"

Nothing happens. Bill-E and Juni keep quiet, but I sense their lack of belief. Ignoring them, I keep talking to the computer, trying to trick it. I don't ackowledge the possibility of failure. Change tack. Start telling it I'm Chuda Sool. "You *will* open — I'm Chuda Sool. You *must* open — I'm

Chuda Sool." Picturing his long, thin face, his browless eyes and cold gaze.

There's a click. Another. A whole series of clickings and whirrings.

The door opens inwards, silent as you please.

I remove my hand and glance back smugly at the astonished faces of Juni and Bill-E. "Oh ye of little faith," I murmur.

We enter.

✠ Darkness. The other rooms were dark too, but I was able to light them with my flashlight. This room's too big. The beam of light is like a pin, showing us almost nothing of the space around us. We can tell that it's huge, but no more than that.

"This feels wrong," Juni says as we stand a few yards from the open doorway, reluctant to press ahead any further.

"It's like we're surrounded," Bill-E agrees, squinting into the darkness.

I sweep the flashlight left, then right. We can't see anyone. But that doesn't mean that people — or other creatures — aren't there. Or that they can't see us.

"Maybe we should come back with stronger flashlights," Juni says.

"If we quit now, we'll never come back," I mutter.

"But we can't see anything."

"Give me a minute. Let me think."

I can't make objects appear out of nothing. But magic is a form of energy. Maybe I can convert that energy into a different form.

Concentrating. Speaking to the magic within me. In a

weird way it feels like I'm two people — the one I've always been, and Grubbs Grady: magician.

"I want to make light," I tell my magical half. "I'd like a big ball of light to appear just above my head. Is that possible?"

In response, I feel energy stream from my hands. It gathers overhead, pulses a couple of times, then transforms into a ball of blinding white light. I gasp with pain, covering my eyes with an arm. "Not so bright!" I hiss, then squint with one eye over the top of my arm. The light has dimmed slightly, but is still painful to look at. "Keep dimming. More . . . more . . . Stop."

I remove my arm. Bill-E and Juni have both covered their eyes. "It's OK," I tell them. "You can look now."

Their eyes are watering when they lower their hands. Juni looks like she's going to be sick. "How did you do that?" she whispers.

"Easy-peasy," I grin.

"You're a freak," Bill-E says. "But a useful one to have around."

"Thanks. Now let's see what we've walked into . . ."

I send the ball of light forward, letting it brighten the farther away from us it moves, until it lights up the entire room. Only it's not really a room. It's a huge, single, cavernous chamber. A bare earth floor. Brick walls that rise up the full height of the building, all three stories of it. No props, furniture, nothing . . . except a tall stone in the center . . . and lots of shapes around it.

Bodies.

"This isn't good," Bill-E says nervously.

"Those look like . . ." Juni croaks, then starts forward.

"Wait!" I cry.

Juni shakes her head. "I have to be sure. They could be old bags or mannequins. I have to check."

"We don't know what's in here with us," I say, losing my nerve slightly.

Juni pauses, looks around, then shrugs. "There's nothing. We're alone. Except for *them.*"

She moves on. Bill-E and I glance at each other. We can't be outdone by a woman. The shame would be too much to bear. So we set off after her, away from the door and the possibility of a quick retreat.

✠ Juni sinks to her knees a few yards from the bodies, staring hopelessly, jaw slack, disbelief in her pinkish eyes. There are twenty or twenty-five of them encircling the stone, the head of one body lying on or under the feet of the next. Emmet's one of the dead. His mother. Kik and Kuk Kane. Their father. Others I don't recognize.

Some of the bodies have chunks ripped out of them or limbs torn loose. Others have cut throats. A few look like they're asleep, but I'm sure, if we turned them over, we'd discover fatal wounds.

Bill-E reels away and vomits, groaning over the mess, shaking his head, trying to deny the reality of this dreadful scene. This is the first time my brother's seen anything like this. It's hard. Not like what you see in the movies. On the silver screen, corpses mean nothing. You know they're not real, just models or actors faking death. You can admire the staging, the special effects, the pools of blood. The grosser it is, the cooler.

But in real life it's sickening. The most distressing sight in the world. Death's always hard to take, but murder . . . slaughter . . . people killed in the name of some disgusting demonic cause . . . spread out like sacks of meat and bone . . .

Juni's taking *deep* breaths. I'm sure she wants to vomit too, but she's keeping the bile down. Just.

Me, I'm a veteran of atrocity. As bad as this is, as much as it hurts seeing Emmet lying there with his throat and stomach slit open, it's nowhere near as bad as when I walked in on my parents and sister and found them torn to shreds. I'm not saying I'm cool with this, or it's water off a duck's back. I'm just better prepared to deal with it than Bill-E or Juni.

I turn my attention away from the bodies, not wanting to dwell on the pain they must have suffered, the tragedy of dying in this callous manner. I study the stone, the focal point of the room. It looks like a Stonehenge monolith. A big chunk of rock jutting out of the ground, mostly smooth, but with a few jagged knobs poking out of it in various places. No writing, at least not on this side. But several gouges run across the middle and near the top, different lengths and depths.

"Some of the bodies have been here a long time," Juni says. She points to a couple of corpses in an especially bad state. Flesh rotting, inner organs dried up, bones jutting through the dry and brittle skin. "This hasn't all happened in the last few weeks."

"No," I agree. "I think this goes back months, maybe longer."

Juni looks around at me. "What the hell's happening?" she sobs. "*Why?*"

Before I can think of an answer, there's a scratching noise behind the rock. Then a sniffing sound, followed by raspy chuckling. Something sticks its head out. Studies us. Then steps into view.

It's a demon. Five long, spindly legs. The body of a giant ant. A long neck and the head of some sort of rabid monkey. No arms, but several small mouths in addition to its main one, sticking out of its body, set on mushroom-like stalks. The mouths are filled with blood-red, dagger-sharp teeth.

The demon gurgles at us. I can read its thoughts — "Fresh meat!"

Juni and Bill-E scream. I scream too, but there's magic in my cry. It hits the demon like a cannonball, knocks it backwards, clear of the stone and bodies. Sends it tumbling across the floor.

"*Run!*" I roar.

Bill-E and Juni don't need to be told twice. They race for the door, howling, terror overriding their other senses. I want to run too. I try to. But the magic stops me. *Not yet*, a voice within me whispers. *You can't let it attack from behind. You'll die if you turn your back on it.*

The demon finds its feet and snarls. It has several bright green eyes, set above and under its main mouth. Some look at the light overhead. The others stay pinned on me. The demon's lips move fast. Inhuman mutterings. I sense magic and prepare myself for an assault, teeth chattering, inching away from the monster, keeping it in sight the whole time.

The ball of light dims, then is quenched, plunging us into blackness.

Bill-E and Juni's screams get louder. The demon shrieks

triumphantly. The sound of scampering feet. My first instinct — turn and run for dear life. But my magic half holds me in place. Makes me listen. The scampering sounds come closer. Closer. Any second now, those teeth will be ripping into my flesh and tearing off chunks of . . .

Sudden silence.

Down! the voice barks.

I drop instinctively and, in response to a second command, stick my legs up in the air. I force magic into my feet, transforming them, directed by the voice.

The demon hits. A wet stabbing sound. My knees buckle, but I hold them straight. There's weight pressing down on me, more than I could naturally bear. I use magic to steady my legs and support the heavy load. The demon's struggling, screeching. Something splashes over my face and neck — blood or bile, maybe both. I scream with fear and hate, then force my feet up higher. The demon chokes, writhes a few more times, then goes still.

I hold my position, wary, in case the demon's faking. But when, after several long seconds, there's no movement, I allow myself to relax a bit and summon a fresh ball of light.

My legs are rigid above me. The demon's impaled on them. I can see two grey, metallic prongs sticking out of the monster's back. My feet, transformed into blades. How cool is that!

"Grubbs!" Bill-E yells.

I tilt my head and look behind me. Bill-E and Juni are standing in the doorway. I see panic in Bill-E's face. He can't see the blades from there. He thinks the demon's feasting on me.

"It's OK," I call, lowering my legs, using my hands to try and push the demon off. When that fails, I use magic to propel it clear, then turn my legs back to their normal form. I stand.

"Grubbs?" Bill-E says, softly this time, uncertain.

I smile at him and Juni. She looks suspicious too. "I killed it."

Bill-E takes a step forward. I increase the brightness of the light so he and Juni can see me clearly, as well as the motionless demon.

"You killed it?" Bill-E echoes, walking cautiously towards me, staring at the dead monster. "How?"

"Magic." I feel weird. I've never killed anything before, apart from flies and other insects. I know this is a demon, and it was trying to kill me, but it's still a strange sensation. I don't feel guilty — I'm glad as hell that I'm not the one lying dead! — but I'm not thrilled either.

Juni steps up beside Bill-E. She's trembling. Brushes strands of white hair out of her eyes. "I've never seen anything like that before," she mumbles. Takes a step towards it. Stops. "Are you certain it's dead?"

"Yes. But others might come. We can't afford to hang around."

"I have to examine it," she says.

"This isn't the time for an autopsy!" I snap.

"I have to make sure there are no wires or engines inside."

"You think thing's a fake?" Bill-E exclaims. "Are you insane?"

"No," Juni says. "To both questions. But I have to be *sure*. If this is real, it changes the entire way I think about the world. Before I accept that, I have to be certain this isn't a clever movie prop that got out of control."

Juni crouches next to the demon. Studies it closely, hands raised defensively in case it leaps back to life and attacks. I move up behind her, also worried about the demon, no longer positive that I killed it. Remembering when I fought Vein and Artery. I could cut them up into pieces, but I wasn't able to kill them. This might be a lesser demon, or I might be more powerful than I was before. Or it might only be wounded, faking death to lure us closer.

Juni kicks one of the demon's legs — no response. She kicks a mouth stalk. It wobbles from side to side, but only from the force of her blow. Slowly, carefully, she pries its main mouth open and peers down its throat. I tense. If the demon's faking, this is the perfect moment to strike. I see the teeth start to come together and I prepare a ball of energy to hurl.

But I'm stressing for nothing. The mouth's only moving because Juni is fiddling with the demon's neck.

"I need a knife," Juni mutters, running her hands over the demon's antlike shell. She looks up. "Either of you?"

Bill-E fishes in a pocket and passes her a small Swiss Army knife. Juni pauses, grimacing, then cuts into the demon's flesh. It's softer than it looks, or else Juni is stronger then she appears, because the blade plunges in up to her hand. She shudders, then carves downwards along the length of the demon's side. Wormlike guts ooze out as she slices, as well as a greyish substance that might be blood. Remembering the spray I caught earlier, I wipe a hand across my face and it comes away wet and sticky with the same grey liquid.

"I'd kill for a shower," I mutter, chuckling darkly at the sick joke.

Juni cuts a long, jagged line through the creature's flesh, ignoring the grey blood and guts, then hands Bill-E his knife. He grimaces and tries to wipe the muck off on his pants. Juni looks at me and grins shakily. "I wanted to be a vet when I was younger," she says — then drives her right hand deep into the demon's stomach.

"This is *so* gross," Bill-E moans.

"It hasn't put you in the mood for liver and kidneys for breakfast?" I ask.

Bill-E's face goes green and he almost throws up again.

Juni searches with her fingers for a minute, then draws her hand out. All sorts of horrible bits and pieces come with it — fleshy and slimy, no wires or mechanisms. Juni stares at her fingers, rubs them together, then tries to clean them by digging her hand into the earth.

"Convinced?" I ask.

"It's impossible," she sighs. "Demons are creatures of myth, the phantasmagorical creations of primitive superstition."

"They're the Demonata," I correct her. "Mankind's greatest enemies. They've existed since before the dawn of our species. They hate us, and love to kill. Sometimes they break through into our universe and the bloodshed starts. That's what happened here." I lock gazes with her. "They've already killed some of us. If we don't warn the others, they'll *slaughter* us all."

Juni nods slowly. "I thought I was so clever," she whispers. "I knew so much about the mind, people, behavior. Now . . ." Her eyes clear and she gets up, businesslike. "Who can we trust?" she asks.

"Dervish," I answer promptly. "But he won't believe us."

"He'll believe *me*," Juni growls, and her face is beautifully stern.

KIDNAP

✠　✠　✠

I keep expecting the worst as we reel back through the warehouse, anxiously retracing our steps, making mistakes and having to backtrack. I'm sure the lights will come on outside, the hole will be discovered, guards will pour into the building to block our escape. Chuda Sool will appear and summon an army of fresh demons. We'll die miserably and be added to the pile of corpses around the stone.

But none of that happens. Apart from the wrong turns, our journey back to the hole in the external wall passes unremarkably. And when we get there, the lights are still dead outside, the guards in their huts, nobody aware of our presence.

"Will we try and fill in the hole?" Bill-E asks.

"That would take too much time," Juni says. "We should just —"

I point at the mudlike mess on the ground. Draw upon the magic. Snap my fingers. "Ubsacagrubbsa!" I quip. And the molten rocks flow upwards, defying gravity. They fill the gap, solidifying within seconds. It's not perfect — there are no in-dividual bricks now, just one large patch of unbroken block — but it should only be noticeable if one of the guards passes up close.

"Nice work," Bill-E says.

"You're growing more powerful by the minute," Juni notes.

"Lets not waste time on compliments," I grunt, I then hurry through the welcome, nighttime darkness of Slawter in search of my uncle.

✠ Even though I'm soaked from head to toe in demon blood, Dervish doesn't believe us. Rather, he doesn't *want* to believe.

"This is a movie set," he insists. "The D workshops are full of amazing demon facsimiles. It wasn't real, just a —"

Juni curses crudely, surprising us all, then points a finger at the startled Dervish. "Don't give me that rot!" she snarls. "You weren't there — *I* was. You didn't see it — I did. It was no piece of movie magic. It was a demon. It would have killed us all if not for Grubbs."

I feel pride welling up inside. Bill-E gives me a dig in the ribs and sticks his tongue out, making sure that my head doesn't get to big.

Dervish stares uncertainly at Juni, finding it harder to dis-miss her protests than mine. That's a positive sign. Chuda Sool hasn't fried Dervish's brain completely.

"It was a real demon," Juni says slowly, keeping her eyes on Dervish's. "I don't know how these things can be real, but they are. It killed Emmet, Kuk and Kik, a lot of others. It —"

"No," I cut in. "That demon wasn't the killer. I think it was just a guard, set there to protect the stone in case anybody got through the rest of the building. There are worse demons than that around — Lord Loss, for one."

"I told you that wasn't —" Dervish begins.

"Shut it!" Juni stops him. "If Grubbs says he saw the demon master, he did. I believe him now. Totally."

Dervish sighs, confused. "What do you want me to do?" he grumbles. "If you've already killed the demon . . ."

"There are more!" I hiss. "The one that killed Emmet. Lord Loss." I glance at Juni and Bill-E. "That was an awfully large room. Why make a room that big for just a few demons? I think more are planning to cross. A *lot* more." I face Dervish again. "You have to stop them. Call the Disciples. Destroy that stone and get all the actors and crew out of here."

"Who are the Disciples?" Juni asks, but I wave the question away, glaring at my bemused-looking uncle.

"I still think it was only . . ." Dervish mutters, then pulls a face. "But I'm not going to argue with all three of you. Let's go back to the warehouse. Show me the demon. If you're right, we'll —"

"If you think we're going back inside that place, you're certifiable," Juni says, beating Bill-E and me to the punch. "Run the risk again? Give them another chance to discover what we're up to, so they can trap and murder us? No way!" She points at the door. "We're out of here. We'll get to safety, call in help — soldiers, police, whoever the Disciples are — then have this place evacuated. I'm not happy leaving the others behind, but it will be safer to help them from the outside."

"That's the sort of plan I like," Bill-E beams. "Run for the hills, tails between our legs — excellent!"

"You're asking me to believe this and flee with you — breaking our contracts, by the way — without any proof, purely on the strength of your word?" Dervish asks sullenly.

Juni stares at him straight. "Precisely."

"That's crazy and insulting," Dervish says coolly. Then winks, looking like my real uncle for the first time in weeks. "Last one to civilization's a rotten egg!"

✠ We take Juni's car. She and Dervish sit up front, Bill-E and I in the back. We drive through the heart of Slawter, heading for the connecting road to the highway. Everybody's silent, staring out the windows. We've seen enough movies to know that this is the part where the bad guys are supposed to show up, block off the road, stop us from leaving.

But we see nobody except a few technicians working on the sets, and they pay no attention to us. Moments later we pass the last building — an old hat store that's been designed to look like it did a hundred years ago — and are on the road to freedom.

"I bet they'll come after us," Bill-E whispers, gazing out the back window.

"No," I say. "By the time they realize we're gone it'll be morning and we'll be too far away for them to catch up."

"Too bad," Bill-E sighs. "I always wanted to be part of a high-speed car chase."

Juni accelerates once we're in sight of the highway . . .

then slows to a stop, though she leaves the engine running. She and Dervish are staring straight ahead.

"What's wrong?" I ask, peering over Dervish's shoulder.

"There's something in the middle of the road," Juni says. "It might be garbage bags."

"Or a body," Dervish murmurs.

I squint but I can't see anything. "Are you sure?"

Dervish nods slowly, then looks at Juni. "Can we circle around?"

"Yes." She licks her lips. "But if it's a person in trouble . . ."

"No way!" Bill-E gasps. "You can't even be *thinking* about getting out!"

"It doesn't sound like the best of moves," Dervish agrees.

"I know," Juni says. "It feels like a trap. But I can't see anybody else. And if there are demons lurking, why wait for us to get out of the car? If they meant to attack, they'd have hit us as soon as we slowed down."

Dervish stares out the windows, then checks the rearview mirrors. "I'll go," he decides. "Keep the engine running. If anything happens — *anything* — slam your foot down on the accelerator and forget about me. Do *not* play the hero. Grubbs?" He glances at me, trusting me to know about life-and-death situations, and how to deal with them.

"We'll do what we have to," I tell him.

"Wish me luck," Dervish mutters and opens his door. Just as he's stepping out, the car shakes wildly. Dervish falls. The rest of us shriek. The engine cuts out. Juni fumbles for the key. The lights go dead. Something hits the car. A cloud of gas. Coughing, I reach for the door handle. Before my fingers find it, gas fills my mouth and nostrils. My eyes close. I groan softly. Then slump over, senses shutting down, figuring the next thing I see when — *if* — I awake will be the jaws of a ravenous demon.

✠ I was wrong about the demon. Instead I wake to Juni slapping my cheeks and calling my name. A far more pleasant sight than one of the Demonata!

"What happened?" I moan, sitting up, shaking my head, ears ringing, the taste of the gas still thick on my tongue.

"We were knocked out," Juni says, going to check on Dervish. I'm lying outside the car, on the road. Dervish is close by, sitting upright, massaging the back of his neck, looking around woozily. No sign of Bill-E.

"Where's Bill-E?" I ask.

"We've been unconscious for forty minutes," Juni says. "I'm not sure what they used on us. It might have been —"

"Where's Bill-E?" I ask again, sharply this time.

Juni looks at me steadily. "I don't know. He wasn't here when I regained consciousness."

I try to stand. Dizziness hits me hard. I stagger and sit down again.

"That happened to me too," Dervish says sluggishly.

"Why are we alive?" I ask. "Why did they spare us and only take Bill-E?"

"I don't know," Dervish says. "It doesn't make sense. This is . . . confusing."

"They might be playing with us," Juni says. "They could have taken Bill-E to use as bait, to lure us back to town, so they could torment us."

"If they did," Dervish says, standing slowly, groaning, "they're smart as hell. I'm not leaving him behind."

"It would be madness to return," Juni says. "We can help him more by —"

"No," I say, standing up like Dervish, fighting the dizziness. "We aren't going without Bill-E."

"But you can leave," Dervish tells Juni. "In fact it would be better that way. Us on the inside, you on the outside. You could spread the alarm and fetch help — if not for us, then for the rest of the people here."

"But . . ." Juni starts to argue, then stops. "No. I can see your minds are made up. I'm not going to waste time trying to talk you out of it. I'll leave, like you suggest. You can give me the names and numbers of anyone you think I should contact. I'll return as quickly as I can, and just pray that's quick enough."

"I like your style," Dervish smiles, reaching out, gently touching her right cheek.

Juni smiles back. Then blinks. "Oh, here, I don't think this has anything to do with Bill-E, but . . ." She picks a small object off the front passenger seat and hands it to Dervish. "I found it nearby when I woke up."

Dervish stares at the object. I see his mouth tighten at the corners. A new cloud of anger rises in his eyes. His fingers clench, then relax. He holds his hand out to me. There's a silver ring nestled in his palm. A flat, circular piece on top, with a gold L inscribed on it.

My eyes shoot up. Dervish and I stare at each other, more astonished than furious. If this ring is what I think it is, demons didn't kidnap Bill-E. He was taken by the *Lambs!*

✠ ✠ ✠

PART THREE
THE LABORATORY

DISCIPLES

✠   ✠   ✠

WE get back in the car and tear out of Slawter as fast as Juni dares drive, Dervish busy on his cell. He makes a series of calls and speaks with six or seven different people. Juni and I listen silently, not understanding everything that he says.

When Dervish finally lays the phone down, he shuts his eyes and massages his eyelids. Juni gives him a few seconds, then says quietly, "I assume the plan is for us to go after Bill-E?"

"Yes," Dervish says.

"And those we left behind? I don't want to be insensitive, but we're talking about the lives of hundreds of people. Is Bill-E *that* important?"

"He is to me." Dervish opens his eyes and sighs. "I'm not forgetting the others. I've convinced two of my colleagues to help us get Billy back. And I'll find another couple to send to the film set."

"Only two?" Juni frowns. "Shouldn't we alert the authorities? Send in more than just a pair of your friends?"

"My *friends* have devoted their lives to dealing with the Demonata for most of their lives," Dervish growls. "The Disciples are people with magical abilities, accustomed to handling messes like this. They'll know what to do."

"But surely, the more backup we provide . . ."

Dervish looks at Juni with a wry smile. "OK. Call the police. Tell them demons are on the loose. Draw little pictures of Lord Loss and —"

"Don't," Juni snaps. "I won't stand for sarcasm, not in my own car."

"Sorry," Dervish says. "But you have to understand, we're on our own, just us and the Disciples. That's the way it's always been. Even if you convinced the police that you were genuine, and they sent troops in, they wouldn't achieve anything. Demons can only be killed by magical means. Human weapons don't affect them, not unless they're wielded by a mage. If the Disciples can't stop the massacre, nobody can."

"But —"

"No more talk," Dervish says, letting his seat back.

"You're going to sleep?" Juni snorts with disbelief.

"I'm going to try," Dervish says. "Unless you want me to drive?"

"No."

"Then wake me when we hit the airport."

And with that Dervish shuts his eyes and dozes.

Juni looks at me in the mirror, astonished. I shrug. "At least he's not acting like a brainwashed simpleton any longer," I say with a smile.

"I think I preferred him when he was!" Juni huffs.

✤ ✤ ✤

✤ We have to wait four hours for a flight, then three hours in the next airport. Dervish makes more phone calls, recruiting a couple of Disciples to go to Slawter, while Juni and I use the restrooms.

I spend several minutes at one of the sinks, splashing water over my face, enjoying the coolness. As I'm dripping dry, I study my reflection in the mirror and frown. Something's not right, but I don't know what. I look much the same as always, skin a touch paler than normal, eyes a bit wider. Yet I can't shake the feeling that something's wrong. Is it my hair? I run a hand through my ginger mop — nothing amiss there.

Unable to put my finger on the problem, I go see how Dervish is getting on, then Juni and I grab a bite to eat.

"You shouldn't worry," Juni says as I nibble distractedly at a BLT. "We'll get your brother back."

"Thanks." I start to smile, but again I'm struck by an uneasy feeling. I glance around nervously — are we being followed? But nobody's watching us. I'm just being paranoid, imagining threats that aren't really there.

✤ A long second flight. Seven hours in the air. Dervish fills Juni in on what's happening. Tells her about the Lambs, the visit from Prae Athim, her interest in Bill-E. Explains about the Disciples, their efforts to stop the Demonata from crossing into our world and slaughtering at will.

Dervish says he knows where the Lambs' main laboratory is

situated. It's part of a vast security complex. Lots of armed guards. Breaking in won't be easy. Very dangerous. He won't blame her if she doesn't want to get involved. Juni waves that away, but she's not entirely happy with the plan.

"You can't know for certain that they'll take Bill-E to this laboratory," Juni says. "What if they place him somewhere less obvious?"

"Then we'll find out," Dervish says flatly. "But this is as good a starting point as any."

I can't shake the edgy feeling I've had since the restroom at the airport. This feels wrong. How did the Lambs know where we were? How did they know we'd be leaving, that they could hit us outside town? And why should Prae Athim kidnap Bill-E in such a dramatic fashion? She must have known Dervish would come after her. She was scared of the Disciples the last time we spoke. Why do something guaranteed to turn them against her now?

I discuss my fears with Dervish, but he dismisses them. "Prae Athim always had a chip on her shoulder about the Disciples. The Lambs don't like playing second fiddle to anyone. Maybe she sees this as their chance to test us. Or perhaps she figured we wouldn't suspect the Lambs, that we'd blame Billy's disappearance on the Demonata. If we hadn't found the ring, we'd never have guessed the Lambs were involved. We were ready to face down the demons. Maybe she hoped they'd kill us."

I remain unconvinced. That doesn't explain how Prae Athim knew about the demons in Slawter. Or how she judged her moment so finely. Or why her people would leave us for the demons to kill, instead of murdering us themselves while we were helpless. This is more involved than it seems. There's a conspiracy afoot. The Lambs in league with the Demonata? Maybe. If Lord Loss or one of his crew offered to give the Lambs the power to reverse lycanthropy, in exchange for a little help getting rid of the meddling Grubbs and Dervish Grady . . .

But that's crazy. We were knocked out. At their mercy. If they'd been working with the demons, they'd have simply handed us over. We'd be dead now, not flying after them in hot pursuit.

Something's wrong, but I can't pin it down, and it's driving me crazy.

✠ The plane touches down. The two Disciples meet us in the arrivals hall of the airport. A man and woman. The man's tanned, tall, and bulky, with short grey hair, dressed in army fatigues. There are letters tattooed on his knuckles — S H A R K — and a small picture of a shark's head on the flesh between his thumbs and index fingers. No surprise when he tells us his name is Shark.

The woman is Indian, dressed in a colorful sari. Old. A kindly face. She walks slowly, with a pronounced limp. Hugs Dervish hard, kisses his forehead, then introduces herself to us as Sharmila Mukherji. She looks familiar, and I realize after racking my brains that Dervish and I watched a documentary about her a while ago.

"I never did like Prae Athim," Shark barks. "I'm looking forward to cutting her down to size."

"But we will have to be careful," Sharmila warns. "The Lambs should not be underestimated. They might not be able to repel us with magic, but they are well versed in other forms of warfare."

"Against us three?" Shark snorts. "They don't stand a chance! It's just a pity Kernel and Beranabus aren't here — it'd be a proper reunion."

Dervish, Sharmila, and Shark smile at each other, while Juni and I share an uncertain look. Then the Disciples quickly discuss their plans and how to proceed. Before setting off, Dervish again gives Juni the option of pulling out.

"To be honest," Juni says, "I'm not comfortable. I'd rather we focused on the problems in Slawter. But if this is where you think the battle is, I'm with you. I won't quit now."

"Fighting words," Shark grins. "You're my kind of gal!" He looks around the airport, sniffs, then nods towards the exit. "Let's go round up some Lambs."

✠ A four-hour drive. Dervish, Shark, and Sharmila discuss the past for the first hour. From what I gather, the three fought together only once before, many years ago, but kept in touch and are close friends. As we progress, talk turns to the present and tactics. Shark has seen the plans of the building and knows the layout of the laboratory, its weak points, where the greatest obstacles will be.

I fall asleep as Shark and Sharmila are discussing the plans, exhaustion catching up with me. I don't dream.

✠ When I awake, we're in the middle of nowhere. Dry, arid land stretches out in all directions. A huge metal and glass building stands ahead of us, ringed by a security fence, dotted with armed guards, sporting a massive antenna on the roof. It reminds me of something. I think I've seen it before, but I couldn't have. I've never been here.

The feeling that something's wrong sneaks up on me again, but I ignore it and focus on the conversation.

"— Electrified, but that won't bother us," Shark is saying. "Once inside the perimeter, we head left. There's a small, disguised door that opens onto a corridor that cuts past a lot of the building — an emergency exit."

"What about the guards?" Juni asks.

"We'll fight them with magic," Shark says. "I would have brought a few weapons along — fight fire with fire — but Dervish vetoed the idea."

"I don't want to harm anyone," Dervish says quietly. "Most of the staff here are just ordinary people doing their job. They won't know about the kidnapping or that we only want to rescue Billy. We mustn't kill them. A person shouldn't be killed just because they're ignorant of the truth."

"You're too soft," Shark grunts, then throws his door open and smacks his right fist hard into his left palm. "Let's do it!"

✠ We stand outside the electrified fence, in plain sight, watching as more guards gather. They cock their weapons, eyeing us critically.

"We're here for Billy Spleen," Dervish shouts. "Tell Prae Athim we know she took him. We'll settle for his safe return. If she gives him back to us, or tells us where he is, we'll leave without a fuss. We don't have to go to war."

A high-ranking guard speaks into his headpiece. Listens to the response. Nods and addresses us through an amplifier. "This is private property. If you try to come onto our grounds, we'll use all available force to halt you."

"War it is then," Dervish sighs. He extends a hand and snaps his fingers at the fence. The wire splits and unfurls, leaving a gap wide enough to drive a bus through. The guards around it yelp with surprise and fall back a few yards. At a signal from Dervish we press ahead, marching but not running. The officer shouts a command. A group of guards raise their weapons and aim at us. Shark and Sharmila mutter a spell. The weapons melt and distort and the guards drop them, crying out that they're too hot to hold.

Gunfire from our right. Much louder than in the movies. Terrifying. I yell and duck, covering my ears with my hands, expecting to be ripped apart by bullets. Juni ducks too. But the Disciples only pause, concentrating hard. After a few seconds I realize the bullets aren't striking. Looking up, I see them dropping to the ground half a yard away. We're surrounded by a magical energy shield that the bullets can't penetrate.

"You could have told me about that," I snap at Dervish as I stand.

"You'd have known about it if you'd stayed awake in the car," he retorts.

We press on.

✠ Shark finds the secret door, and we slip inside. I'm delighted — the air was red with bullets around us, and I heard Sharmila grumble that she wasn't sure the shield was going to hold much longer. Shark shuts the door once we're all in and uses magic to seal it in place, so the troops will have to blast through to enter.

We hurry down a long, brightly lit corridor. As with the outside of the building, there's something familiar about it. I'm sure I've seen it before. This is déjà vu of the highest order. It's really starting to bug me.

Guards spill into the corridor as we come to the end. Shark roars as they fire upon him, then throws himself at them, scattering them like a bowling ball knocking apart a set of pins.

We slip through the gap and race down a staircase. Guards are firing at us from all directions, but the shield holds. At the bottom of the staircase we wait for Shark to catch up. The volume of gunfire increases. "We could use some help," Dervish grunts at me. He's sweating.

"What do you mean?"

"Break those up," he says, nodding at the guards. "Stop them from all firing at once."

"How?" I frown.

"Magic, dummy!"

"But I can't —"

"Of course you can," he snaps. "Just focus."

I feel uneasy about it, but I do as Dervish says, set my sights on a group of guards and direct a ball of magic at them. Seconds later, unnatural energy floods through me, smashes into the middle of the group of guards and sends them flying in all directions.

"Way to go!" Juni whoops.

I grin at her, pleased with myself, then disrupt more of

the guards, causing as much chaos as I can, careful not to seriously injure anybody.

We advance through a series of corridors, up and down staircases, Shark leading, the rest of us — besides Juni — providing cover from the guards. Eventually we come to a door that's operated by fingerprint recognition.

"This is your field of expertise," Sharmila says, winking at me.

"No problem." I step forward, lay my hand on the panel and trick the computer into believing I'm Prae Athim, much like I did back in the D workshops. The door slides open. We enter a large, dimly lit room. Grim brick walls. Lots of cells, cased off by hard glass panels, like those in the movie *The Silence of the Lambs*. Several lab technicians in white jackets. A handful of guards.

And Prae Athim.

The scientist is scowling at us, her dark eyes like a couple of drill bits. "You're trespassing on private property," she growls.

Dervish laughs. "Sue us!"

"This is outrageous," Prae Athim says. "You have no right to come in here."

"*You* have no right to steal my nephew," Dervish retorts.

"I don't know what you're —" she starts to say, but before she can complete the denial, we hear a voice shouting from one of the cells.

"Dervish! Hey, Dervish, I'm in here! Help!"

Prae Athim glares at one of the technicians close to her. "I told you to dope him so he couldn't speak!"

"I did," the underling whimpers.

"Magic is stronger than drugs," Sharmila laughs. She smiles at me. "I thought they might try something like that, so I sent out a wake-up call when we came in, guaranteed to raise just about anybody who was not dead."

I race to the cell where the call came from. Bill-E's inside, smiling shakily. "What took you so long?" he says flippantly.

"We weren't going to bother coming at all," I reply, turning the glass in front of me to water, stepping back as it splashes over the floor and washes away. "But Dervish said every family needs its simpleton."

"Charming!" Bill-E huffs, then steps through the puddles of water and hugs me hard. "Thanks for not leaving me here," he whispers. I can hear tears in his voice.

"I'd never leave you behind," I whisper back, then push him away before things get any more mushy.

"Did they harm you?" Dervish asks, standing where he is, keeping a wrathful eye on the quivering Prae Athim.

"Listen to our old maid of an uncle!" Bill-E sniffs, winking at me. "Nah, they gave me some nasty injections, but they didn't have time to do much else. You came too quickly — ruined their well-laid plans."

"That's a habit of mine," Dervish laughs. He stares coolly at Prae Athim. "Now, we just have to decide what to do with —"

"No," I say softly, interrupting. Dervish glances at me, one eyebrow raised. "No," I say again, shaking my head, staring at the cells, the technicians, Prae Athim, Bill-E. My head's clearing. All the little bits that didn't add up . . . that seemed out of place or too familiar . . . I'm starting to see it now. Bill-E helped me make the breakthrough. Provided the jolt that shattered the spell. He called Dervish his uncle. Nothing wrong there — Dervish *is* his uncle. Except Bill-E doesn't know that.

"What's wrong?" Dervish asks.

"Wait," I mutter, waving his question away. Thinking hard. Cutting through the web of lies and crapola.

These cells don't just *look* like the set from *The Silence of the Lambs* — this *is* Hannibal Lecter's institution. And now I realize now where I've seen the building before. In James Bond movies. There are bits from several of the films, pieced together roughly.

I step away from Bill-E, dizzy, fighting to hold on to my train of thought. "Grubbs," Juni says, concerned, stepping towards me. "Are you OK? Can I help? Is there —"

"Shut up!" I shout, breaking through the labyrinth of untruths, rapidly, one lie falling after another, mental dominoes toppling quickly.

I'm a mage, not a true magician. I was only able to draw upon my potential in Slawter because of all the magic in the air. There's no magic in this laboratory, so how come I'm able to unleash great energy bursts and turn glass into water? The same goes for the Disciples. They shouldn't have so much power here.

All the logical hiccups and flaws reveal themselves in quick succession. The Lambs turning up at just the right moment to knock us out and kidnap Bill-E. Dervish handily knowing the location of the main laboratory was. Prae Athim taking Bill-E there. Shark so conveniently having seen the plans of the building.

Sharmila knew that I'd opened the fingerprint-operated

door in the D workshops — but we hadn't told her about that. In the second airport, Juni referred to Bill-E as my brother — but she doesn't know that we're related.

And in the restroom, the first time I became aware that something was wrong. I get it now, what I saw but couldn't put together. My reflection was *clean*. It had been all the time, even before I washed my face. Clean skin, hair, clothes. No grey demon blood. But I got soaked in the D chamber. I never washed the blood off. It should have been caked on at the airport, just as it should be caked on now. But it wasn't and it isn't, because . . .

"None of this is real!" I scream, startling everyone around me.

"Grubbs," Juni says softly. "Calm down. You're losing control."

"You're not real!" I shout. "None of you are!"

"What's wrong with him?" Dervish snaps at Juni.

"I don't know. Maybe he —"

The magic part of me whispers something. It's been quiet all this time, even while I thought I was working magic. But now it breaks its silence and tells me what to say. Ignoring the chatterings of the figures around me, I bellow out loud, words of magic and power. Prae Athim's face contorts with hatred. Demon eyes glare at me. She shrieks, as do all the scientists and guards — but it's too late.

The walls of the cells bubble. The human Lambs turn into demons, then fade. A red haze comes down around Dervish and the others. Magic phrases trip off my tongue. Pain washes over me. I fall to my knees but keep on shouting, ripping the vision to pieces. The redness thickens. Fills the room, block-ing out everything, humans, demons, all.

I utter the final words of the spell and wearily close my eyes.

Everything goes silent.

PART FOUR

✠ ✠ ✠

DEMONS-A-GO-GO

WAKEY WAKEY

✠　　✠　　✠

DERVISH snoring. When I hear that, I know I'm back in the real world — there's no mimicking a dreadful, pig-choking noise like that! I open my eyes and sit up, groggy, head pounding, utterly confused but no longer ensnared by the dream reality of the laboratory.

I'm in a small, dark room, chinks of light sneaking in around the edges of a dusty old set of blinds. Propped up on a bare wooden floor. Dervish and Bill-E spread out next to me. Both asleep.

"Dervish," I mumble, shaking him hard. No answer. I shake him again, hissing his name in his ear, not too loud in case anybody's on the other side of the door. Still no response. I roll up his eyelids with one hand and snap my fingers in front of his eyes with the other. He carries on snoring.

You were all dreaming the same thing, the magic part of me whispers. *In their minds, they're in the Lambs' lab. They can't wake themselves. You'll have to use magic to bring them back.*

It tells me the words to use. I murmur them softly, feeling magic flow out of me, into my uncle and brother. They stir. Bill-E moans. Dervish grunts something about an armadillo. Their eyelids flicker and they struggle awake.

"What's happening?" Bill-E groans.

"Where are we?" Dervish asks. "Where's Prae Athim? Sharmila? Shark? The —"

"That was bull," I cut in, steadying him as he tries to stand. "Easy. Don't make any noise. We're probably under guard."

"I don't understand. What . . . ?" He stares around, forehead creased.

"It was a dream. The kidnapping, meeting up with the Disciples, the lab. None of that was real. It was all fantasy."

"Don't be crazy!" Dervish snaps. "I know the difference between . . ." He stops. Thinks about it. His jaw drops. "Bloody hell. It had me fooled completely."

"Me too, for a while. But parts didn't add up. There were mistakes."

"The lab," Dervish says slowly. "It looked familiar. Now I know why — I got the image from Franz Kafka's book, *The Trial*."

"Kafka?" I frown. "It looked like buildings from James Bond movies. And the cells were straight out of *The Silence of the Lambs*."

"What are you talking about?" Bill-E says. "The cells were like something in a sci-fi flick, all those control panels and lasers."

"We provided our own dream variations," Dervish says wonderingly. He rises, panting, and leans against a wall until his legs support him. He staggers to the blinds and parts a few slats. Peers out. Then looks at us. "We're still in Slawter. We never left. Grubbs is right — it was all an illusion."

Dervish walks around the room, giving his head time to clear, flexing his legs and arms. "I forgot how cunning the Demonata are. They're masters of deception. They found out we were leaving, or they had a barrier in place to stop anyone getting out. Blocked us with magic. Created an insane scenario that seemed logical to us. Since our minds were active and focused on the dream — thinking that was reality — we couldn't wake up."

"Why not simply drug us?" Bill-E asks.

"They're demons. They don't work that way." Dervish chuckles. "I can't believe I fell for it. Walking onto the planes without tickets. Breezing through customs, nobody asking to see our passports."

"I didn't spot that," I wince.

"What about you, Billy?" Dervish asks. "Notice anything out of place?"

"No," Bill-E says, scratching his head. "Although I did think it strange that some of the nurses weren't wearing any . . ." He coughs and blushes.

"They wanted us out of the way," Dervish says, "so they subdued us. They could have killed us, but I guess they want us around for the finale. If Lord Loss is masterminding this, he won't want to slaughter us while we're sleeping. He'll want to make us suffer first, so he can feast on our pain and gloat."

"We have to get out of here," I pant, getting up, fighting off a wave of dizziness. "We have to stop them. Get everybody out. Call the Disciples."

"What about Juni?" Bill-E asks, and Dervish and I flinch, only now realizing that she isn't with us.

"They're probably keeping her in another room," Dervish says.

"Why?" Bill-E frowns.

"I don't know. It doesn't matter. There isn't time to think about it."

He strides to the door and presses an ear against it. I can tell by Bill-E's expression that he's going to push Dervish about Juni. I slip up beside him and whisper, "Dervish didn't say it, because he didn't want to freak you out, but Juni's probably dead. That's why she isn't here."

Bill-E stares at me, ashen-faced. "But she was in the laboratory . . ."

"So were a lot of people. That doesn't mean anything." I squeeze his arm. "Dervish cares about Juni a lot, but he can't think about her now. We can't either. We can hope for the best, and if we're lucky we'll find her, sleeping like we were. But if she's not . . . if the worst has happened . . . we have to overlook it for now. We have ourselves to worry about. And all the others."

Bill-E trembles, but nods reluctantly. I squeeze his arm again, then help him to his feet. When he's able to walk, we edge up behind Dervish, who's still listening intently at the door. "Anything?" I ask.

"No. But that doesn't mean there's no one there. Or no *thing*."

"We can't wait in here forever," I note.

"True." Dervish looks over his shoulder at me. "Ready to fight?"

I crack my knuckles. "Damn straight."

"Then let's go for it."

He turns the handle and slams open the door.

Nobody's outside. We creep along a damp, musky corridor. We're in one of the town's original buildings. It hasn't been renovated. Holes in the walls, rotting floorboards, broken windows.

"How much of that dream world was real?" I ask Dervish, trying to calm my nerves by focusing on something other than the possibility that we might run into a team of demons any second. "Sharmila and Shark — do they really exist?"

"Yes," Dervish says. "And pretty much the way we saw them — or at least the way *I* saw them. From your viewpoint, was Shark wearing army fatigues? Sharmila a sari?"

"Yes."

"Then that much we shared." Dervish pauses and looks at me. "How did you know it wasn't real? What tipped you off?"

"Lots of little things. But it was when . . ." I glance at Bill-E. "What did you say to Dervish when we broke you out?"

Bill-E thinks a moment. "I'm not sure. Something like, 'Hey, neighbor, what took you so long?'"

"I heard you say something else, something you shouldn't have said. That let me fit the different pieces together."

"What did I say?" Bill-E asks.

"It's not important," I lie, not wanting to tell him that in my version he knew Dervish was his uncle.

"You were clever to break the illusion," Dervish says. "Even if I'd twigged, I'm not sure I could have woken up. A spell like that will normally divert you down another path when you start to suspect something, lead you into the middle of another dream."

"Maybe it has," I laugh edgily. "Maybe this isn't real and we're still lying on a floor somewhere, asleep."

Dervish grunts dismissively. "I'm not *that* gullible. This is the real world. We're awake. I'm sure of it." But he looks around nervously all the same. Then his gaze settles on me again. "If we come through this, you and I need to have a talk."

"What about?"

"Magic. You're doing things you shouldn't be able to. I want to know how."

"No big mystery," I shrug. "I'm just drawing magic out of the air, putting it to good use, like when we fought Artery and Vein."

"Hmm," Dervish says, unconvinced. He licks his lips and focuses. We're almost at the back door. I can hear voices outside. But they're human voices and they fade quickly — people walking past.

"What now?" Bill-E asks. "Do we try driving out of town again?"

"No," Dervish says. "We have to alert the others. Tell people what they're up against. They might not believe us, so we'll have to be firm. Get them out of here, even if we have to force them. Fight if necessary — and I expect it will be. If we're lucky, we'll only have to worry about Chuda and his human accomplices."

"And if we're unlucky?" I murmur.

"Let's not think about that," he says, then opens the door and walks out to face whatever hell awaits.

ASSEMBLY CALL

✠   ✠   ✠

O N the outskirts of Slawter. Proceeding slowly, Dervish slightly ahead of Bill-E and me, one hand held palm up, trying to determine whether or not there's a barrier in place. He said we should determine the lay of the land before raising the alarm. No point trying to herd dozens of people out of town if they're going to be knocked out by a magically enforced shield.

"Why aren't we hungry?" Bill-E asks, checking the date on his watch. "We've been asleep for . . . hell on a Harley! Six days! We should be ravenous but I don't even feel hungry."

"Trust you to be thinking about your stomach at a time like this!" I snort.

Dervish laughs gently. "No, it's a good question. The answer's simple — magic. We were cocooned from the demands of the real world. Hunger and thirst will hit us later, if we make it out, but right now we're still operating by the magical rules of Slawter."

"Is there anything magic can't do?" Bill-E asks.

"Not much," Dervish says, then draws up short. His fingers are trembling. He moves his hand left, right, left again. "Can you feel it?"

"No," Bill-E frowns.

"Yes." I take a step forward, sniffing the air. It doesn't smell different, but it feels wrong. I raise a hand like Dervish, slide it forward, sense power building against it.

"No further," Dervish says. "We don't want to disturb the fabric of the barrier — it might tip off our enemies."

"What is it?" I ask.

"In nontechnical terms, a bubble of magic. They've sealed off the town. Enclosed it within a magical sphere, like putting a giant glass bowl over everything." He frowns. "No demon is powerful enough to create a barrier this size, not in our universe. They're using the stone you saw in the D workshops. It must be a functioning lodestone, a reservoir of ancient power. There aren't many left in the world. The magic drained from most of them centuries ago. Others were deliberately destroyed, to prevent them from falling into the hands of demonic mages.

"This is worse than I thought. With the power of a lodestone at their disposal, they can build a tunnel. Dozens of demons can cross and run riot within the barrier. Stay as long as they like. Nobody will be able to escape."

"We have to stop them!" Bill-E gasps. "We can, can't we, Dervish?"

"Of course," Dervish says wearily, lowering his hand. "If we shatter the lodestone, the bubble will burst. But now that we know about it, the Demonata will have increased security around the warehouse. They're not stupid."

"We have to try," I say quietly. "We can't stand by and let people die."

"You're forgetting our earlier conversation," Dervish says with a bitter smile. "The Disciples often let people die. In a situation like this, we'd normally sit back and let the De-monata run their course. We don't have the power to stop them. Better to conserve our strength and fight them when we have a chance of winning."

"But this is different," I growl. "We know these people."

"That's not enough of a reason to get involved. I've had to sacrifice friends to demons before."

"Don't tell me you mean to —" I start to explode.

"Easy," Dervish calms me. "We won't stand by idly. We can't. Because you're right, this *is* different. We're caught up in it. If we don't find a way out, it's not just the cast and crew of *Slawter* who'll perish — we'll die too."

✠ Heading into the heart of town. Dervish says there might be another way out of this mess — burst through a small section of the bubble, creating a temporary gap through which we can flee. But we're not powerful enough to do it ourselves. We need to pin a demon against the bubble, then explode it with magic. By focusing the energy generated, we should be able to blast a hole through the barrier, which we can keep open for a while, allowing people to slip out.

Should. No guarantees.

One of our main problems will be getting a demon in the right place, at the right time. We can't just march into the D workshops and ask one of them to come to the barrier with us.

But before that, we have to figure a way to convince the

rest of the crew and cast that we're not crazy, their lives are in danger, demons are real, they have to trust us if they want to live. To that end, we're heading for Davida Haym's offices. If she's innocent — bloody unlikely — Dervish hopes to recruit her and use her to issue a general alarm. If, as we suspect, she's in league with the Demonata, he plans to make her confess in public, to persuade the others.

It's hair-raising stuff, sneaking through town, ducking down side alleys, keeping out of sight. We don't know who our enemies are. Dervish doesn't think many humans will be working for the demons, that most of the people here are innocent. But we can't be sure who to trust. We know a few of the traitors — Chuda Sool and Tump Kooniart, the guards who were with Kuk and his father when they disappeared, probably Davida. But there will be more. We can't expose ourselves and risk raising the alarm.

I suggest making ourselves invisible. Dervish vetoes the idea. "Powerful demons can sense magic being used. We've been lucky so far, but every time one of us draws on the power in the air, we risk pinpointing our position."

So we steal through town unassisted by magic. Luckily, although it's afternoon, Slawter is quiet, not many people about. We make it to Davida's offices unnoticed and let ourselves in. One of her secretaries is usually stationed at the front desk, but our luck holds — the chair is vacant. We slip past and into the main office, the hub of operations, from which all orders flow.

Davida isn't here. The office is empty. Lots of papers,

small demon models, a miniature set of the town, maps on the walls with scores of dates, names, times, schedules. But no Davida Haym.

"Go through the drawers," Dervish says, hurrying to one of the many file cabinets in the room. "Look for anything that might give us an advantage — plans, a list of demons, spells, whatever."

"You think she'll keep details like that in unlocked cabinets?" Bill-E asks.

"No," Dervish sighs. "But it'll keep us busy. And you never know — we might get lucky."

Rooting through drawers, pulling out folders, glancing through the pages, then discarding them, scattering them across the floor, not caring about the mess we're making.

I'm halfway through a drawer when Bill-E makes a shushing sound and hurries to the door. He listens for a second, then nods — people are coming. Dervish and I move up next to him, taking cover behind the door, crouching low so as not to be visible through the upper panels of glass in the office wall.

Footsteps. Two people talking. The door opens.

"— *have* to get it right," Davida Haym says, stepping into the office. "This is a one-time deal. If we blow it, we won't . . ." She spots the mess and stops.

"What the hell?" Chuda Sool says, stepping up beside her.

Dervish springs to his feet. His right hand comes flying up, fingers curled into a fist. He punches Chuda's jaw like a professional boxer. Chuda grunts and spins aside, smacking hard into the glass of the upper wall, cracking it. Bill-E and

I leap on Davida as she screams. We pull her down and cover her mouth with our hands. She tries to bite but we jam our hands down more firmly.

Dervish closes in on Chuda, who's dazed but still on his feet. Chuda tries to block Dervish's next punch, but it penetrates, grazing the side of his head, not connecting as firmly as the first blow, but knocking Chuda back a few more inches. I always knew Dervish was stronger than he looked, but I've never seen him in this sort of kick-ass mode before. It's cool!

Chuda grabs a paperweight from Davida's desk and swings it around, but Dervish blocks his arm and knocks it aside. Chuda roars and gets the fingers of one hand on Dervish's throat. Dervish lets him squeeze, cool as ice, sizing him up. Then he pummels a fist into Chuda's stomach. Chuda grunts. His fingers loosen. Dervish takes a step back, judges the angle, then takes one final crack at his opponent's jaw. Chuda's head snaps back, his eyes flutter shut, and he slumps to the floor.

Dervish turns away from Chuda, panting lightly. His eyes fall on Davida, still struggling beneath Bill-E and me. He jerks his head at us. We slide off. Davida starts to sit up, spluttering furiously. Before she completes the move, Dervish puts a foot on her chest and pushes her back down. Stands over her like a triumphant gladiator, fixing her with a glare evil in its intensity.

"Now, lady," he snarls, "it's time for you to talk. And you're going to tell me exactly what I want to hear." He moves his foot up to her throat. "You can be sure of it."

✠ "You have no right to do this," Davida says sourly. Dervish has allowed her to rise. She's sitting in her plush leather chair, glaring at us. "When I tell security what you've done, you'll be in so much —"

"We know about the Demonata," Dervish snaps. "Lord Loss and his familiars. The barrier and the lodestone in the D workshops. You can't fool us any longer. So talk."

Davida pinches her lips shut. I know Dervish thinks she's working with the demons, but he's not sure. I guess he figures it's best to assume the worst and treat her harshly. He can apologize later if she's innocent.

"Don't think I won't do terrible things to you," Dervish says softly. "I obey human laws when it suits, but break them without hesitation when I must. The only reason I haven't gone to work on you is the boys. But I'm five seconds away from sending them out to the next room and doing whatever I have to to get answers."

"You don't know what you're interfering with," Davida snarls, betraying herself, confirming our worst suspicions. "This is way beyond anything you can imagine."

"You underestimate my imagination," Dervish smiles icily.

"These are real demons, you fool! They can do things you wouldn't believe. If you mess with them, you'll wind up —"

"I've been messing with the Demonata for decades," Dervish interrupts. "Now tell me your story. How deep are you in this? What did they promise? Power? Magic? Eternal life?"

"They promised nothing except what I asked for — a great movie."

Dervish frowns. "We're past that stage. Your lousy movie cover is blown. I want to know the real reason why —"

"*Cover?*" Davida laughs contemptuously. "It was never a *cover*. I'm making the greatest horror film ever. A movie with real demons, doing what real demons do, captured on film — what better reason could there be than that?"

Dervish's frown deepens. "You're telling me that was the trade-off? You helped the demons cross to our world provided them with all the victims you could, and they agreed to be filmed? It was as shallow as that?"

"You know nothing about moviemaking," Davida sneers. "Life is shallow. It's meaningless. Life passes and is forgotten within minutes. But movies endure. A film outlives everyone involved. If it's good enough. If it's magical."

She leans forward intently. "You think I'm evil and you're probably right. I brought all these people here, knowing they'd die. But we all die in the end. Pointless, forgettable deaths. We fade and it's like we never existed. We come, we live, we die, and that's that. Not much of a story, huh?

"But that's about to change for you, me, everybody here. We'll become part of history. I'm making a movie which will survive as long as the human race itself. Demons will attack ... kill hundreds of people in unimaginable ways ... and I'll capture it all on camera. Splice it in with the other scenes I shot. Make the most shocking horror film ever. I'll be notorious, yes, feared and despised. I'll be imprisoned, maybe executed. But I'll be *remembered*. And so will the others. And that's the most any of us can hope for."

She stops, breathing heavily, face flushed.

"She's loco," Bill-E says. "How come she wasn't locked up years ago?"

Dervish shakes his head in wonderment. "So you planned to let these people be butchered in the name of art, so you could film the massacre and turn it into entertainment. That's a new one. I've seen crazy mages bring the Demonata into our world for all sorts of reasons — but never to break box office records."

"You don't get it," Davida laughs. "This is immortality. It will put us up with the ranks of the great. We'll mingle with the giants of history — Caesar, Alexander, Napoleon. The world will always want to see this film, to experience true terror, to get as close as they can to the reality of the demonic."

"You're deluding yourself," Dervish says. "There won't be a film. Even if you capture the footage, you won't live to edit it. The Demonata will kill you along with the rest of us. You'll be a brief news item — nothing more."

"No," Davida insists. "We have a deal. I give them you, they let me make my film."

"Do you have that in writing?" Dervish chuckles, then stops. "What do you mean, you give them *us*?"

"I've spent the last several years recruiting demons," Davida says. "I got a few lesser demons involved, once I laid my hands on the lodestone and they saw that I was serious, but I needed a demon master. By myself, I could only use the stone to create a brief window between universes. I knew a demon master could help me use it to build a tunnel, letting many more demons through and giving them plenty of time to cavort.

"The trouble is, demon masters are hard to contact. I managed to find one — Lord Loss — but he wasn't interested. I pushed ahead anyway, determined to make the best of what I had. Then, a few months ago, Lord Loss sent one of his most trusted servants and offered his services — *if* I could lure you and the two boys to the set. Lord Loss hates you. He wanted you to be here, to suffer horribly before he personally ripped you to pieces."

"So you came to Carcery Vale to ensnare me," Dervish says bitterly. "Did you cast a spell? Mess with my mind?"

"Of course," Davida smirks. "It wasn't that difficult, or so I've been told — I didn't do it myself. Your brain was all over the place. Quite easy to manipulate. You fell into our trap without any complications. I'm just surprised you recovered your senses now. You weren't supposed to wake until tomorrow, when the bloodshed was in full flow. Still, it doesn't really matter. Your timing's slightly ahead of schedule, but only just. It's far too late to make a nuisance of yourself."

"What do you mean?" Dervish growls.

"You don't know?" Davida giggles with delight. "I did think it strange that you were here, grilling me, instead of . . . I thought you hoped to use me as a shield, to bargain your way out. But you really don't know, do you?"

"What the hell are you —" Dervish starts to shout, but is cut short by a voice outside, amplified by a loudspeaker.

"Ten minutes," the voice says. "Will everyone please assemble immediately outside the D workshops. Ten minutes to showtime, folks!"

Dervish stares at Davida, face whitening. She giggles

again. "It's the final scene, Grady. When the demons break through and hell erupts. We brought it forward once you found out the truth — we couldn't keep you comatose indefinitely. The actors and crew think the heroes in the movie will save the day. But that's not how it's going to work. I've got a surprise up my sleeve. Dozens of demons who aren't playing by the rules of monster movies, who don't have weak spots, who aren't going to be thwarted by a clean-cut movie brat with a cool haircut and a dazzling smile."

Davida looks at her watch and smiles serenely. "Nine more minutes. Then Lord Loss and his familiars burst out of the D warehouse and kill just about every living soul in town." She brings her hands up and claps slowly, to emphasize each word. "Lights! Camera! *Slawter!*"

THE REAL STARS
OF THE SHOW

✠   ✠   ✠

ERVISH rushes out of the office, leaving a laughing Davida and unconscious Chuda Sool behind. Bill-E and I hurry after him. "Shouldn't we have tied Davida up or knocked her out?" I pant, running fast to catch up with Dervish.

"No time," he barks.

We race through the mostly deserted streets of Slawter. Dervish spots a group of people making their way to the assembly point. He roars, "Get out! Go back!" They stop and stare at him oddly.

"There's been an explosion!" Bill-E yells, lurching up behind us. "They think it's a gas leak. The entire gas system's been compromised. There could be further detonations anywhere within town. We have to get out. *Now!*"

"Good one," I compliment him as the panicked group turns and heads west.

"We need to think about this logically," he gasps, face red from running. "If we tell people that demons are going to kill them, they'll think we're nuts."

"So we make it a gas leak instead," I say nodding. "Get them moving away from the danger zone. You hear that, Dervish?"

"Whatever," he grunts. "But in another few minutes we won't have to tell them anything — they'll see the demons themselves."

✠ We round a corner and approach the gigantic D warehouse. A huge crowd has gathered outside. Most of the people are at the southern end, but some spill around the east and west wings of the building. There are cameras everywhere, on tripods and cranes, in the hands of cameramen mingling with the crowd, a couple on top of the warehouse roof. I guess the cameramen are part of Davida's inner circle, wise to the Demonata; otherwise she couldn't trust them to man their posts when the chaos erupts.

Several of the crew have megaphones and are directing the crowd. Dervish storms over to the nearest one — a young man with a ponytail — grabs the megaphone, and shouts into it, "Gas leak! There have been explosions! Everybody out! We have to evacuate *now!*"

Uncertain mutterings among the crowd. People stop talking and stare at Dervish. He's running up and down, repeating his message, gesturing in all directions, telling people they have to head for the outskirts of town immediately.

Before anyone can move, a large man steps forward with a megaphone of his own. It's Tump Kooniart. "Ignore that lunatic!" Tump roars. "It's Dervish Grady. We fired him last week. He's trying to disrupt proceedings to get back at us. Guards — seize him! The boys too!"

Security guards move forward. Dervish curses and tosses his megaphone aside. "Enough of this gas-leak crap," he mutters. "Time to open their eyes."

Dervish says something magical and points at the guards closing in on him. They float up ten feet into the air, with yells of alarm and fear. All around us, jaws drop. Eyes fix on the floating guards, then on Dervish, who looks like a man charged full of electricity.

Dervish touches a couple of fingers to his throat and addresses the crowd, his voice far louder than it was with the aid of the megaphone. "You're all going to die. Davida Haym has struck a deal with demons. *Real* demons. They're going to break out of the warehouse in a couple of minutes and kill everyone. Unless you flee now, you're doomed."

"Ignore him!" Tump Kooniart screams. "He's lost his mind!"

I see Bo and Abe close behind their father. They look worried, scared, incredulous, like most of the people around us.

"Real demons?" Tump snorts. "Madness! He's trying to wreck the shoot. He —"

Tump Kooniart chokes, drops the megaphone, falls to his knees, face purple, hands clawing at his throat and mouth.

"Don't kill him," I whisper in Dervish's ear.

"He deserves to die," Dervish snarls, looking completely unlike the gentle man I've lived with all these months.

"Maybe," I say, voice trembling. "But we don't have the right to kill people. We're trying to save them, even those who don't deserve it."

Dervish snorts, but breaks the spell. Tump Kooniart breathes again.

"Listen to us," I shout, using magic to amplify my voice. "I know it's hard to believe, but you can see the guards floating overhead. You can hear our voices, even though we're not using any equipment. Your lives are in danger. You have to run now or else —"

"Enough!" Davida Haym screams, her voice even louder than mine or Dervish's. The guards fall back to earth, some injuring themselves badly. Davida's standing behind us, a groggy Chuda Sool by her side. Her eyes are blazing. "You're not going to ruin my movie! Cameramen — are you ready?" Dozens nod and shout that they are. "Sound?" Davida cries.

Dervish raises a hand to stop her. Before he can, he's spun aside by a magical force. It's not Davida's work. Doesn't look like Chuda's doing it either. There must be a powerful, hidden mage somewhere in the crowd.

"Sound?" Davida shouts again and this time there's an answering bellow. "All right. Let's dispense with the countdown and cut to the chase. All of you inside the warehouse — it's time to make your grand entrance.

"*Action!*" she roars, and the hounds of hell are unleashed.

✤ The giant door in the middle of the southern wall of the warehouse explodes outwards. Those nearest it are caught by flying splinters, some as long as my arm. Most go down screaming, though a few aren't able to, torn apart by the shrapnel.

Stunned silence from those not struck by the debris of the blast. Everybody's staring at the wounded and dead. Wondering if this is real or part of the movie. They live in a make-believe world where anything can happen and nobody is ever really hurt. Their senses tell them this is different, it's not part of a script, they should run. But the moviemaking part of their brain is trying to figure out how the explosion was arranged and how the scattering of the splinters was timed so as not to harm anybody — struggling to convince themselves that those on the ground are acting, the blood isn't real, it can't be.

Dervish is back up on his feet. Staring at the hole in the wall like the rest of us. The explosion created clouds of dust around the doorway. As they clear, a figure glides forward from within the warehouse. Pale red skin, lumpy, no heart, eight arms — who else but the ringmaster himself, Lord Loss?

"Alas," he sighs, looking around sadly. "Here we all are. Bound by chains of blood and death. No way out. Doomed. Dervish tried to warn you, to save you, but he failed. Here you are trapped. Here you will die."

One of the cameramen moves in for a close-up. "Yes," I hear Davida murmur. I glance back. She's speaking into a microphone, directing the cameraman. "His face first, then pan down to the hole in his chest. I want to see those snakes slithering."

Lord Loss gazes without much interest into the camera. He smiles slightly, then runs his eyes over the crowd, judging their mood, taking in their expressions, most more confused than terrified. "Ah," he notes. "You do not believe. You think this is part of the film. That I am a movie prop." He chuckles. "It is time to burst that bubble of misperception."

He moves to one side. I glimpse other shapes behind him. Eyes. Tendrils. Teeth. Claws. Fangs. "Now, my darlings," Lord Loss whispers.

The demons spill out in their dozens, each one more mis-shapen and nightmarish than the last. A variety of vile mon-sters, spitting bile, oozing pus and blood, screeching and howling with malicious glee. They collide with the shocked members of the cast and crew closest to the building. Cut into and through them, severing limbs and heads, disemboweling, biting, and clawing.

Realization hits the masses swift and hard. A single scream rings out. Then a volley of them. Panic sweeps the crowd. A stampede develops, everyone wanting to get away from the demons, trampling over one another, the weak going down in the crush, dying beneath the feet of their workmates. An-archy at its most destructive and terrifying.

Lord Loss laughs, and his laughter carries over the sounds of the screams. I'm rooted to the spot, unable to react, heart jackhammering, not wanting this to be happening, wishing I could be anywhere in the world but here.

I see the cameraman who moved forward turning away to capture the scenes of mayhem. "Not yet!" Davida snaps. "Stay on the hole. Give me a close-up."

The cameraman steps right up to Lord Loss's chest, ma-neuvering his camera to within an inch or two of the writh-ing, hissing snakes. He moves his head from behind the camera to check something — and one of the snakes strikes. It lashes out from within the hole where Lord Loss's heart should be. Sinks its tiny fangs into the cameraman's left cheek. He yelps, drops his camera, and tries to pull away. But the snake has a firm hold. It yanks him closer, so his face plunges into the hole. And now all the snakes are biting. The cameraman's arms and legs thrash wildly, then go still. He falls away a few seconds later, his face a blood-red map of bites and rips, skin flailed, bones cracked, brains dribbling down his chin.

"No!" Davida gasps. "He hadn't finished the shot! They shouldn't have . . ."

She stops and studies the demons tearing into the humans. They're drawing no distinction between the intended victims and the collaborators, dragging down cameramen and other technicians as well as the unsuspecting members of the cast and crew.

"*No!*" Davida screeches. "We had a deal!"

Lord Loss looks at her sneeringly. "I do not make deals with fools. I promised you chaos, which you and your underlings could film, but I never said I would spare any of you. You simply assumed — and assumed wrong." He smiles at me. "Greetings, Grubitsch. Such a pleasure to see you again. I will take much satisfaction from your long, slow, painful death."

"Not today!" Dervish bellows, and suddenly he's by my side, right hand raised. He fires off a bolt of energy at Lord Loss. The demon master deflects it, but is knocked sideways. "Come on!" Dervish snaps at me and Bill-E. "We have to get out of here."

"But what about . . . ?" I gesture at the fleeing people.

"We'll summon them when — if — we blast a way out," Dervish says. "The best thing they can do is split and flee. That will delay the demons and buy us some time."

"But —" Bill-E begins.

"No arguments!" Dervish barks. "Follow me now, or so help me, I'll leave you for the bloody Demonata!"

With that he turns and flees south, sidestepping the stunned, frozen Davida Haym. Chuda deserted her when he realized they were going to perish along with those they'd planned to sacrifice. I'm not sure where he thinks he can run to or hide, but he fled anyway.

Davida can't move. She's weeping, seeing all her dreams of immortality go up in flames. I'd like to say I feel sorry for her, but I don't. All I can think right now is, "Serves you right, you crazy old cow!"

Then Bill-E and I are past the desolate producer, following Dervish through the maze of streets and alleys of Slawter, the screams of the dying and yowls of the demons rising all the time.

✠ Twisting and turning, Dervish in the lead, no apparent route in mind. He stops in the middle of a street. There are doors on either side of us. Handy for a getaway if we're attacked. "Are you OK?" he asks us.

"Any reason we should be?" I reply calmly, hiding my terror as best I can.

Bill-E says nothing. He looks like a shell-shocked soldier. As awful as I feel, I think Bill-E feels a hell of a lot worse.

"Billy?" Dervish says softly. "Are you with us? Are all the lights on in there?" He taps the side of Bill-E's head.

"They killed them," Bill-E wheezes, his lazy left eyelid snapping open and shut at great speed. "I saw a thing with . . . it looked like a tiger . . . but bits and pieces sticking out . . . it killed Salit. He tried to stop it. He didn't know it was real. He was acting his movie part, where he was a big hero. But it cut him down the middle and —"

"We don't have time for hysterics," Dervish growls. "Be a man and help us fight, or go babble somewhere until the demons find you and kill you."

I hate him for saying that, but I know he's only doing it for Bill-E's sake. Cruel to be kind and all that guff.

Bill-E glares at Dervish, anger driving the fear away. "I'm not hysterical," he says stiffly.

"Glad to hear it," Dervish says. "Now listen and listen good. Lord Loss is the only demon master. The rest are his familiars, or others Davida roped in. Some are stronger than us, but most aren't. We need to capture one of the weaker demons and use it to get out."

"And the other people?" I ask quietly.

"We'll take as many as we can," Dervish promises. "If we're successful, I'll send a telepathic signal and let all the survivors know where we are."

"Why not do that now?" I ask. "Arrange a meeting place and tell them to go there. It would give them more time, a better chance."

Dervish shakes his head. "Those who were working for the Demonata would receive the message too. They'd go running to Lord Loss — try to save their own foul lives by selling out the rest of us."

"OK," I mutter. "So how do we catch a demon?"

Dervish scratches his left cheek nervously. "Bait," he says softly. And his gaze settles on Bill-E.

✤ I don't like it. Hell, I hate it! But it's the quickest, easiest way. We're up to our eyeballs in trouble. We have to take risks.

We leave Bill-E standing in the middle of the street, twisting his hands, face crumpled with fear. He trusts us but he's terrified. I would be too in his shoes.

"If anything happens to him . . ." I whisper to Dervish.

"It won't," Dervish says solidly. "Now don't talk — watch."

A minute passes. Two. Screams fill the air, a chorus of agony and anguish. Every hair on my body is standing upright. I have to keep my teeth parted, afraid I'll grind down to the gums if I don't take care. Part of me wants to run, make for the barrier, force a way through, forget everybody else. Save your own skin, it whispers. Dervish and Bill-E are the only ones who matter. Convince them to leave with you. Let the others look after themselves.

I ignore the treasonous, selfish voice — but only with an effort.

Movement at the end of the street. Several figures come racing around a corner. Dervish and I tense, ready to unleash a burst of magic, then hold it back when we see that the figures are children. Bo Kooniart, Vanalee Metcalf, three others.

"Run!" Bo screams at Bill-E. "We're being chased! Get the hell out of here, you moron, before —"

"Bo!" I yell. "Over here." She stops, panting, eyes wide with terror. "Quick!"

"But there's —"

"I know. Trust us. We can stop it. But you have to —"

"Here it comes," Dervish interrupts.

I look left. A demon with the body of a giant bee is humming through the air after Bo and the others. As it gets closer I see that it has a semi-human face, except with bee eyes, and more teeth than any human I've ever seen. Magic flares within me. I stretch out a hand in the direction of the bee demon.

"Not yet," Dervish says. "Let it get closer . . . closer . . . *Now!*"

Together we channel magic and unleash it. Twin bolts of energy strike the demon sharply, knocking it across the street, away from the children. It smashes into the wall on the opposite side. As it slumps to the ground, Dervish runs towards it. I follow, caught up in the moment, acting instinctively.

The bee shakes its head and starts to rise, buzzing angrily. Dervish grabs a wing before it gets out of reach. Yanks it down. The bee lashes out at him with a stinger the size of a large kitchen knife. He ducks. I scream and smash an elbow into the bee's semi-human face. Its teeth bite deep into my forearm, but I jerk my arm free before it can do serious damage.

As I grab the bee with my uninjured arm, I feel Dervish's magic burn into the demon. It makes wild buzzing sounds. Thrashes, trying to break free, snapping its teeth, stabbing at him with its stinger. He holds on tight. I do too. I head-butt the bee, letting magic shoot through my forehead, intent on sizzling the demon's brains.

"Not too much!" Dervish pants as the demon goes slack. "We want it alive." He stands, sliding both arms around the bee. "Let's keep it like this and —"

"*Monster!*" a voice screams and suddenly there's someone beside us. A hand shoots by my head. A fist buries itself deep in the demon's chest, then comes ripping out, dragging guts

and yellow blood with it. Stunned, I fix on the face of the as-
sailant — and my heart leaps joyfully.

"*Juni!*" I yell, releasing the bee's head, throwing my arms
around her.

Juni Swan hugs me hard, then steps away, staring at
the demon, then her fist. "How did I do that?" she croaks. "I
felt something inside me. It was power, but I don't know
where . . ."

"Hi," Dervish says quietly, letting the dead demon drop to
the floor. He smiles crookedly, then slips his arms around
Juni and buries his face in her neck. "We thought you were
dead," he half-sobs.

"I was . . . dreaming, I think," she says. "Bill-E was kid-
napped. We rescued him. Then we were attacked by ninjas
and had to go to a mountain in search of their lair." She
shakes her head. "I woke up in a small room. I came out and
saw demons. I ran away. Then I saw you. I thought the bee
was going to kill you. Something exploded inside me. Before
I knew it . . ."

She stares at her fist again, a look of astonishment on
her face.

"Seems you have a talent for magic after all," Dervish
chuckles, then sighs. "But you timed it badly. We wanted
this one alive." He quickly explains his plan to her and the
children, who've crept across. Bo seems to be less shaken
than the others. She's trembling fiercely and her face is
white with fear, but she's in control of her senses and listens
intently.

I use magic to heal my wounded arm, and watch Bo cautiously. Her father was one of the collaborators, but that's

not her fault. I'm pretty sure she didn't know about his pact with the Demonata. Bo was never anything worse than a spoiled brat. You don't deserve to be killed for that.

Dervish finishes outlining his plan. "So Grubbs, Juni and I will pull back, leave you kids here, wait for another demon to come along, then . . . ka-blooey!"

"*Ka-blooey?*" Juni repeats, raising an eyebrow.

"I liked comics when I was a kid," Dervish says with a shrug.

"How are we going to get the demon to the barrier?" Bo asks, and though her teeth chatter, her voice sounds normal.

"Grubbs and I will drag it there," Dervish says. "Juni can help."

"But —"

"Here she goes," Bill-E groans. "Always has to have her say!"

"Shut up, shrimp-breath!" Bo snaps, then appeals to Dervish. "I don't want to be a troublemaker. I just want to get out of this alive. But it's what you said about how you were going to alert everybody and tell them where to come." She pauses.

"Go on," Dervish says kindly, though if I was in charge, I'd tell her to put a sock in it. She's being a drama queen, trying to grab the attention. Typical Bo.

"Well," Bo says hesitantly, "if you're able to use telepathy, I was wondering . . . can demons do the same?"

Dervish stares at Bo, then nods slowly. "Some can."

"So," Bo continues, "if you catch a demon, and it realizes you're dragging it off to the edge of town to kill it, won't it call for help? And bring a load of other demons down on top of us?"

Dervish scowls. "She's right. It'll take several minutes to

get to the barrier from here. If the demon summoned help, we'd never make it."

"Can't we knock it unconscious?" Juni asks.

"Perhaps. But if it gets out a shout . . ."

He falls silent. Bo looks at me smugly, but I'm too impressed to bear her any ill feelings. She's not entirely brainless, I'm reluctantly forced to admit.

"I have a suggestion," Bo says. She's stopped trembling. Confident. On a roll.

"I'm all ears," Dervish says with a wry smile.

"Why don't we lure a demon to the barrier before you go messing with it? Trick it into chasing after us. It wouldn't call for help if it didn't know its life was in danger."

"We have a genius in our midst," Dervish says, smile widening. Bo beams like an angel. Despite myself, I have to laugh. She'll be more unbearable than ever after this, but right now that doesn't seem like such a bad thing.

"There's only one problem with your proposal," Dervish says.

"Problem?" Bo frowns.

"Running's dangerous. If there's a demon hot on your heels, you can't concentrate on what lies ahead. Very easy to run into another demon, or a pack of them. We can't control the situation if we do what you suggest. And control is vital. Grubbs and I *must* reach the barrier. If we don't, everybody dies. We can't risk running into a trap."

Bo mulls that over, starts to speak, goes silent, then says very quietly, "What if the rest of us did the running? What if you and Grubbs went to the barrier and we tried to lure a demon to you?"

I blink, astonished. I never thought I'd hear the spoiled Bo Kooniart make a suggestion like that. What she's proposing is close to self-sacrifice. Without us, she and the others won't stand much of a chance against the demons.

"You know what you're saying?" Dervish's voice is grave. "You know the risk you'd be taking?"

"Of course. But it doesn't seem like we have much of an option, does it?"

"I'm not doing it!" Vanalee protests, bursting into tears. "I want to come with you, Mr. Grady! Please don't make me go after demons!"

"I won't make anybody do anything," Dervish says. He looks at the other children. "Bo's risking a great deal for us. Will anybody volunteer to save her, or are you going to leave her to face the demons by herself?"

The three children look at one another. Two raise shaky hands. The third hangs his head.

"OK," Dervish says. "Now all we have to do is arrange a meeting place, so you know where —"

"I'll go too," Bill-E interrupts.

"No!" I yell.

"I have to." He smiles thinly. "I'm not magical like you and Dervish. There's no benefit in me coming with you. I can do more good with Bo and the others."

"But —"

"He's right," Dervish says. I look at my uncle, unable to believe he'd let Bill-E go like this. But his eyes are dark and firm. This isn't easy for him, but he's going to let Bill-E go anyway. I start to protest, but then I realize why Dervish is doing this — it wouldn't be fair to let Bo and the others volunteer and not put forward one of our own.

"I'll go," I whisper. "You take Bill-E."

"No," Dervish says. "I need you at the barrier."

I shake my head. "You can kill a demon without me. And you have Juni to help. The others will stand a better chance if I go with them."

Dervish hesitates.

"We can both go," Bill-E says.

"No. You're sticking with Dervish, no arguing." I lower my voice so only Bill-E can hear. "I don't want him to lose us both. And you're his son — you're more important to him than I am." I hate lying to Bill-E, but if it saves his life, it will be worth it.

"OK," Bill-E says miserably, after a moment of tormented consideration. "But I'll kill you if you don't come back alive."

"All right," Dervish says. "We're wasting time, and we don't have much of it. Grubbs can go with the others. Now, you know the old hat store we passed when we tried to drive out of here?" I nod. "Make your way to that, then head due west. We'll be waiting. Come as fast as you can." He looks at Juni. "Ready?"

"Don't you think I should go with the children?" Juni says nervously.

"No. They're as safe with Grubbs as they would be with you. Safer."

"Well . . . I don't like it . . . but if you think that's best . . ."

"It is." Dervish looks at me steadily. "See you soon — and that's an order."

Then he, Juni, Bill-E, Vanalee, and the boy head west to safety. Dervish is the only one who keeps his sights set firmly ahead. The others all look back, faces dark with doubt. They think they won't ever see us again.

I want to call after Bill-E and tell him we're brothers. I don't want to die without telling him the truth. But my mouth's dry. My throat's tight. I can't.

I stare at Bo and the others. One's a boy a year or two older than me. The second is a girl a few years younger. I don't know either of them. I think about asking their names, then decide it's better not to know.

"Are you all ready?" Bo asks, taking control, even though I'm the one who should be in charge. We nod silently and turn towards the sounds of bloodshed and mayhem. Pause a terrified moment. Then silently jog back into the death den of the Demonata.

THE CHASE

✠   ✠   ✠

I want so much not to be doing this. One half of me is screaming bloody murder at the other half, telling me I'm crazy, I should run, protect my own neck, and damn the rest. But how could I leave Bo Kooniart to save the day? I'd never be able to live it down.

We pass from one street to another. No sign of the De-monata, though the cries of the dying and the roars of demons are everywhere. I'm sweating buckets. Can't stop shivering. I never knew I could be this scared. After all, I've face Lord Loss before. But it's even scarier this time. I'm starting to understand that fear is like cancer — you can beat it back, but if it returns, it can be worse than ever.

We turn a corner and find three demons feasting on a dying man, tearing into his flesh, gulping down bloody chunks as if they were marshmallows. One of the demons is shaped like a short elephant, another a giant cockroach, the third a huge slug that's been partially melted. Vomit rises in my throat, but I force it back.

As the elephant-shaped demon moves aside to chew on a piece of gristle, I recognize the unfortunate victim. It's Chai, the mime artist. Even in his death throes he's remained true to his role. He isn't screaming aloud, but is instead miming weakly. It would be hilarious if it wasn't so tragic.

I want to help Chai, but it's too late. Even as I take a step forward, he stiffens, makes a few last feeble gestures, then goes still.

I study the demons again as they continue to strip the corpse of flesh. They don't look like they're especially swift on their feet. I check with Bo and the others. They're terrified, but each nods to show that they're ready.

"Hey!" I try to shout, but the word comes out as a squeak. I try again, but my mouth is as dry as a lizard's butt.

"Some hero you are," Bo mutters. Then she cups her hands over her mouth and bellows, "*Hey!*" The demons look up. "Come and catch us, uglies!"

She turns and runs. The rest of us follow. The demons shriek and give chase.

✠ Running as fast as I can. With my long legs, I quickly pull ahead of the others. Start to leave them behind. Feeling good, like I'm going to survive. Even if the demons catch up, they'll have to chew through the other three before getting to me. Maybe they'll stop there, happy to have one human each, leaving me free to race to safety and . . .

But that's not the plan. I'm supposed to be helping, not outpacing the others. I keep the speed up for a few more seconds, wrestling with my conscience. Then I curse and slow down, letting Bo and Co. catch up with, then slightly overtake me.

I look back. The demons are close, only ten or twelve yards behind. They can move a lot faster than I thought. If I don't stop them, they'll be on us long before we make it to the edge of town, never mind the barrier beyond.

I stop and force magic into my fingers. Try to think of the best way to stall them, when they suddenly stop, stare at me hatefully, then turn and shuffle off.

"What the . . . ?" I squint at them, thinking this must be a trick, but they keep going.

"What's happening?" Bo asks. The three of them have stopped. They're staring dumbly at me and the departing demons.

"I don't know," I mutter. "Maybe they sensed my magic and decided there were easier pickings elsewhere. Or —"

Something barrels into the boy whose name I don't know. He screams once, then is silenced. The girl and Bo leap away from him. I see a squat, long demon, like a dog, but with spikes sticking out all over, and no legs. It's munching on the boy's head. I start towards them. Come to a halt when I hear a familiar voice high above me.

"You did not think I would leave you to the whims of my familiars, did you, Grubitsch?" I look up and spot Lord Loss, hovering above the roof of the building to my left. He descends slowly, gracefully. "I gave orders for you, your uncle, and brother to be spared. I plan to finish you Grady boys off by myself."

Lord Loss comes to within half a yard of the ground and

stops, his eight arms extended, smiling viciously. "What now, poor Grubitsch?" he murmurs. "Have you the strength of character to fight a demon master, or will you run like a cowardly hyena?"

"*Run!*" I roar, then race away from him. Bo and the other girl hurriedly join me.

Lord Loss laughs and sets off in pursuit of us, savoring our fear and flight. He doesn't have the slightest clue that I'm running for a reason other than sheer terror, that I'm trying to lure him into a trap. He glides along after us, calling to me, the usual crap, telling me how desperate the situation is, how I'm going to let myself down, the pain I'll suffer, the tears I'll shed. He says I'll betray Dervish and Bill-E, abandon my friends, beg for mercy.

I know he's messing with my mind, trying to stoke up my fear, to wring more misery out of me. But it's hard to ignore him. I feel myself losing hope, seeing the future through the demon's eyes. Part of me wants to surrender and accept a swift, painless death. And perhaps I would — except I remember his look of hate when I beat him at chess, his vow to make me suffer before he killed me. There will be no quick, easy death if I fall into Lord Loss's hands.

A strange skittering sound. I look over my shoulder. The dog demon is chasing us too. It's almost upon us. It uses its spikes to move, a bit like a centipede crawling, only a hell of a lot quicker. It has a head like a dung beetle's, but dog-sized.

"Go, Malice," Lord Loss says, and the demon leaps high into the air, coming down on Bo's head, mouth opening wider than its narrow body, fangs glinting.

I shoot a bolt of magic at the demon called Malice and

knock it sideways. It squeals, hits the ground, twists sharply, launches itself at my face. Without thinking, I turn my right hand into a blade, drop to one knee and slash at the demon's underbelly. Malice sees the threat but can't change direction. My hand slices its stomach open from neck to tail. It's finished by the time it hits the ground, entrails spilling out, whining feebly as it flops into the dust.

"Fool!" Lord Loss snorts at his dying familiar. "I am ashamed that one of my servants should be defeated so pitifully." He spits on the dying demon, then looks at me and smiles. "You are stronger than the last time I saw you fight. You were unable to kill Vein or Artery then, yet here you have killed two just as powerful. You must be feeling confident, like you could even defeat *me*?"

"Maybe," I growl, magic bubbling up within me, picturing the demon master dead at my feet, tasting the triumph of revenge.

Lord Loss chuckles. "Do not delude yourself, Grubitsch. You are not *that* strong. A demon master will always outrank and outpower a human."

"Dervish beat you," I sneer. "He fought you on your own turf, and won."

Lord Loss's features darken. "That was not a fight to the death. He had only to get the better of me in battle. He could not have killed me. Just as you cannot kill me now."

Lord Loss reaches out with all eight arms, pauses, twists slightly, and beckons. The girl whose name I didn't ask for goes flying towards him, screaming. I try to pull her back, but before I can, she's in the demon master's embrace.

"Poor little Karin," Lord Loss sighs. "You had such fine

dreams. A movie career, marriage, children." The girl screams, struggling to break free. I try to pry her out of Lord Loss's grasp, but he deflects my magic easily, then kisses her. She goes quiet. Stiff. Her skin turns grey as he sucks the life out of her. I hear bones cracking. Her feet jerk a few times, then stop.

Bo's crying. She sinks to her knees, defeated, staring at the demon master as he drains the girl of the last vestiges of life. I want to give up too. But I know I won't be killed as smoothly as this if I do.

"Come on!" I roar, grabbing Bo's arms, yanking her to her feet.

"I can't," she sobs.

"You can!" I shout, pushing her ahead of me. "Run! Now! Or I'll kill you myself!"

Bo curses me but does as I command, lurching forward, running blindly, wiping tears from her eyes. I look back at Lord Loss. He casts the girl's ruined body aside and smacks his lips. "Karin was a tasty little girl," he says with relish.

"I hope you choke on her!" I scream in retort, then wave a hand at the building above him and cause the outer wall to explode. It showers Lord Loss with bricks and chunks of cement, taking him by surprise, driving him to the ground. I know I haven't killed him, but I've delayed him, and that's all I wanted. Turning, I race after Bo, screaming at her to run faster, trying to judge how much distance is left and what our chances are of making it to the barrier alive.

✠ Lord Loss is soon on our trail again, scratched and bruised but otherwise unharmed. He congratulates me on the way I brought the wall down on him, but adds that if I'd thought of it a bit earlier, I could have saved poor Karin. Making me feel guilty, as though I'm to blame for her death.

I ignore the demon master. Turn corners wildly. Race through the streets of Slawter. I stumble occasionally, fall hard twice, and scrape my hands and knees. But I keep ahead of our hunter and force Bo on, making her stay ahead of me so I can see when she falters and roar at her for support.

Two more of Lord Loss's familiars join him. One is the giant cockroach I saw earlier. The other is even more familiar. A young child's body but with an unnaturally large head. Pale green skin. Balls of fire instead of eyes. Maggots for hair (it used to be cockroaches). Small mouths set in both its palms. The hell-child, Artery.

"No need to introduce you two," Lord Loss says. "Although, if you are interested, this fine specimen" — he nods at the cockroach — "is called Gregor."

"Very amusing," Bo snorts, but I don't get the joke, so I just keep on running, saving my breath for a scream of triumph. Or a death cry. Whichever proves more appropriate.

✠ Finally, as I'm starting to think we've lost our way, I spot the old hat shop. Seconds later we dash past it and are out of town, racing across soft, grassy ground. Lord Loss and his familiars pursue us casually, taking their time, confident we can't escape.

"You should have tried to hide," Lord Loss taunts me. "You stood a better chance that way. This was a poor call, Grubitsch. It will cost you your life. Bo's too. I will make you watch while Artery eats her from the inside out. That will be the last thing you see in this world."

Looking for Dervish and the others, but there's no sign of them. My heart sinks like the Titanic. I'd be able to see them if they were here. No trees or bushes for them to hide behind. It's open ground. Maybe I got the meeting place wrong, but I doubt it. I think they've fallen. They didn't make it out of town. They ran into some bad-ass demons and are dead now. Just like Bo and I soon will be.

"Where . . . are . . . they?" Bo gasps. She looks more petrified than ever.

"Keep going," I reply. "Find the barrier."

"But —"

"Do it!" I roar, then whirl and yell a spell at Lord Loss and his familiars, prompted by my magical half. The ground in front of the demons bursts upwards. Blades of grass thicken, lengthen, and entwine. They form a net that wraps around the startled demons, tightening, choking them, holding them in place.

I look for Bo. She's still running. I jog after her, keeping one eye on the Demonata, hardly daring to hope. And I'm right not to. The grass around them turns brown . . . red . . . burns away. Seconds later, Lord Loss is free and his familiars are soon clawing their way out. There are blades of green jammed into many of the cuts on Lord Loss's body, but unless they turn septic and he dies of disease much later — some hope! — he's going to be fine.

I try the same spell again, but this time Lord Loss is ready, and with a wave of two hands the blades of grass bend downwards and spread out, flattening, not getting in the way of the demons.

"Fool me once, shame on you," Lord Loss says. "Fool me twice . . ." He pulls a smug expression. "But nobody has ever fooled me twice, Grubitsch. And you will not be the first."

Bo yells with pain and surprise. My gaze snaps forward. She's come to a halt and is struggling with an unseen force, arms and legs jerking slowly, as if caught in a web. Moments later she frees herself and falls backwards.

We've reached the barrier. Nowhere else to run. With an empty feeling in my gut, I stop and face the approaching demons.

Showdown.

BATTLE

✠　　✠　　✠

ARTERY and Gregor spread out to the left and right of their master, falling a couple of yards behind. They're here to make sure we don't escape, and perhaps they'll get to kill Bo as a bonus. Neither will be allowed to harm me. Lord Loss is keeping me for himself.

"Grubbs," Bo whimpers.

"I know," I say softly.

"What are we going to do?"

"Be brave. Fight."

"But I don't know any magic."

"Just do what you can." Eyes on Artery and the cockroach. Trying to believe it's not hopeless. If I can pin one of them to the barrier and kill it, Bo and I can escape. Too bad we can't take anyone with us, but I mustn't think of that now. I have to focus on getting us out alive.

"Did you forget about the barrier, Grubitsch?" Lord Loss sniggers. "You are slow to learn. I would have thought, after running foul of it once, you would have had more sense than . . ." He stops, frowning. "But you are not stupid. A cunning boy, as I learned to my dismay the last time we clashed. Might you have had another motive for coming here?"

He's close to the truth. I have to act now, before he makes the connection. My eyes flick from Artery to Gregor. I settle on the baby — smaller, hopefully easier to manipulate. With a magical cry, I unleash my power. Artery shoots forward, into the air, wailing with alarm, propelled towards the barrier. I step closer to the spot where he's going to hit, readying myself to kill the hell-child.

But then he stops in midair. I feel a force working in opposition to mine. I scream a phrase of magic and tug harder. Artery jolts forward another yard, stops again, then falls to the ground. He scuttles back to his master, hiding behind him like a child seeking shelter behind a parent.

"That was a very nice attempt, Grubitsch," Lord Loss murmurs. "You had me tricked until almost the very end. I should have known you had an ace up your sleeve. Dervish must have told you how to create a rip in the barrier. You planned to kill my sweet Artery and skip out of the party early." He tuts mockingly. "That was rude. I shall have to . . ."

I hear noises in the background and spot people running towards us from the town. Lord Loss looks around, casting his eyes over the various faces, searching — as I am — for Dervish. But my uncle isn't part of the crowd. He's not racing to my rescue. These are just ordinary, terrified movie folk. They won't be any help.

"More victims," Lord Loss laughs. "See how they run towards me? Perhaps, from a distance, I look like an angel. Should I pretend to be good? Sweep them to my breast, shower them with kisses, only to turn vile and make my true intentions known when it is too late for them to escape?"

I focus on the cockroach. I try to pitch him at Lord Loss, hoping to knock the demon master off-guard, then hurl Gregor or Artery at the barrier. But the demon doesn't even slide an inch off balance.

"No, Grubitsch," Lord Loss says. "We will have no more of that. Leave my familiars alone. Your battle is with me, not them."

"Then come on!" I scream. "Step up if you think you can take me! What are you waiting for? Do you want to reduce me to tears before you attack? Afraid to fight me on even terms?"

Lord Loss's face goes dead. The snakes in the hole in his chest stop hissing. "So be it," he whispers, rising three feet higher into the air, arms spreading outwards with a slow, dreadful, majestic grace.

"Grubbs," Bo mutters.

"Not now!" I hiss, trembling all over, preparing myself for whatever Lord Loss is about to launch against me.

"But . . . over there . . . it's . . . I think I can see . . . *Dervish!*"

That word startles me so much, I look away from the threat of Lord Loss. Thankfully, the demon master is also taken by surprise, and instead of piercing my defense and finishing me off, he too glances aside.

Bo is pointing off to my right. At first I don't see what she's gesturing at. The land looks devoid of life, just grass and weeds. But then I notice the air shimmering slightly. The shimmer intensifies, thickens, then fades to reveal . . .

Dervish! And just behind my uncle, between him and the barrier — Bill-E, Juni, Vanalee, and the boy whose name I don't know.

"An invisibility shield," Lord Loss groans. "I don't believe I —"

A wind blows up out of nowhere. It smacks hard into Lord Loss, driving him backwards, bowling him and Artery over.

"Grubbs!" Dervish yells, focusing on the wind, veins stretched across his face like ridges of blue putty. I know instantly what he wants. Pointing at Gregor, who has been unaffected by the gale, I shout a word of magic. The demon flies forward, jaws gnashing together in a mixture of hate and fear. He strikes the invisible barrier. Sticks. Dozens of tiny legs kick at thin air as he tries to tear himself free.

"Juni!" Dervish shouts. "Kill it like I showed you!"

Juni steps up to the struggling cockroach. She makes a fist and takes aim at the brittle shell of its stomach. Then she pauses and half turns away, lowering her fist. She's smiling. She starts to say something, but before she can, one of Gregor's hairy, spindly legs strikes the back of her head. She falls with a startled cry, tries to rise, then slumps, dead or unconscious.

My first instinct is to rush to her aid, but I ignore it. Instead I look for Artery. Concentrating on the fire in the hellchild's eye sockets, I magically rip the flames out. As Artery squeals and slaps blindly at his eyes, I transport the flames to inside Gregor's stomach — like cutting and pasting on a computer.

I hold the flames tight for a second, letting them increase in strength but keeping them compact. Gregor is frothing at the mouth, glowing from the inside out. I flash the cockroach a wicked grin. Then, snapping my fingers for emphasis, I release the flames and they erupt in a ball of destructive red and yellow fury.

The demon explodes with a cry of delicious agony. There's a crackling, throbbing sound. Then a jagged line appears in the air around the demon's remains, a rough semicircle of discolored light — a hole in the barrier!

"Get out!" Dervish barks at Bill-E and the others. The wind is still blowing, but Lord Loss and Artery have stopped tumbling backwards and are facing into it now, the demon master furious, Artery confused, waving his childish hands at his empty sockets, trying to ignite fresh flames.

As Vanalee and the boy race to safety, Bill-E hurries to Juni's side. He turns her over, checks quickly, then shouts, "She's alive!"

"Then take her with you!" Dervish roars, struggling to maintain the wind.

Bill-E hesitates — I can see that he wants to stay and help — then grits his teeth. Propping Juni up, he slides his hands under her armpits and drags her through the hole. As they exit, the quality of light changes and it's as though I'm looking at them through a thin, semi-translucent veil.

Bo scrambles to the opening but stops and looks back at the crowd racing towards us. She's panting hard, squinting. "My father and brother. I can't see them."

"Forget them," I growl.

"I can't."

"You must. They're —"

"I'm going back for them!" Bo cries.

"No!" I shout, but she sets off regardless.

My left hand rises. Magic flows. Bo comes to a forced stop. She turns her head and looks at me pleadingly. "Grubbs," she whimpers. "Let me go. I have to do this."

"But you'll die if —"

"Probably," she interrupts, "but not necessarily. Maybe I'll find and rescue them." She shrugs helplessly. "I have to try."

"But your father was working with the demons. He helped bring this on us."

"He's still my dad. And Abe did nothing wrong. Besides get on your nerves, like I did," she grins.

I grin back and reluctantly release her, knowing I don't have the right to deny her, figuring I'd probably do the same in her place. "Don't spend too long looking for them," I warn her.

"I won't," she lies. And then she's gone, racing past the people escaping town, leaving me to marvel at how poorly I judged her.

I wish Bo silent luck, then block her from my thoughts and step up beside Dervish. I want to bolt through the hole in the barrier after Bill-E and the others, but my uncle needs me. My magical half shows me how to link up with my uncle. As I add my power to his, the force of the wind increases. Lord Loss slides backwards again, straining against the wind, but — momentarily at least — losing ground.

"You could have let me know you were here," I growl.

"Couldn't risk tipping off Lord Loss," Dervish disagrees. "We were lucky. You normally can't fool a demon master with an invisibility spell, but he was so focused on you, he didn't see through it."

People from the town spill past us, then through the hole,

called to safety by Bill-E, who's laid Juni to one side and is now directing the survivors.

"You sent the message to everyone?" I ask.

"Yes. As soon as I saw you coming."

"How come Bo and I didn't get it?"

"I excluded you. I —"

"— didn't want to tip off Lord Loss," I finish for him.

"Sorry," Dervish says.

"Don't worry about it."

The wind suddenly dies away. Lord Loss straightens himself.

"What does that mean?" I ask.

"We should get the hell out of here."

There are still people running and limping towards us from the town, chased by demons, some missing limbs, many bleeding and screaming, all terrified but hopeful. Because Dervish told them to come. He said this was their way out. He promised.

"You're staying," I note.

"Until the hole starts to close," Dervish nods.

"You'll know when that's about to happen? You'll escape in time?"

"I'll know. As for whether or not I'll be able to escape . . ." He jerks his head at Lord Loss, who's started to glide back towards us.

"OK," I decide, proud of my courage but at the same time dismayed. "I'll stay too. We'll buy the survivors as much time as possible."

Dervish smiles. "Did I ever tell you I loved you, Grubbs?"

"No."

"Good. I hate sentimental crap like that."

Then Lord Loss shrieks and fire engulfs us.

✠ Dervish spits out words of magic, and the flames evaporate before they have time to burn through our skin. But Lord Loss uses those few seconds to sweep across. With a cry of hate, he propels himself at Dervish, whips him off the ground, and drags him high up into the air, all eight hands lashing and ripping at him.

No time to worry about my uncle. Artery is only seconds behind his master. Races at me on his tiny feet, flames in his eyes bright and vicious again, the teeth in his three mouths gnashing menacingly.

I wait until Artery reaches me, then drop to one knee and shoot a hand out. I grab his throat. Squeeze the cartilage hard. Crush it. Toss him aside. Choked gurgling sounds. Artery brings up his hands to repair the damage. I step towards him, set on finishing him off. Before I can, another demon bursts onto the scene. It's shaped like a monkey with several heads and has been chasing humans out from town. When it sees the hole in the barrier and spots me battling with Artery, it comes barreling at me.

I glimpse claws and fangs. Whirl away. A blast of magic hits my left shoulder. My arm goes numb. When I look down, I realize it's been cut clean off. It lies on the ground nearby, singed and twisted.

"Grubbs!" Bill-E screams as the monkey demon closes in for the kill.

"Stay where you are!" I yell, kicking the demon away, magically stopping the blood pumping from the gash where my arm should be. I bark a command and the earth at the demon's feet explodes, throwing it backwards. While it's recovering, I grab my arm and stick it back in place, blasting magic at it. Severe pain as flesh, muscles and bone knot together, but I use more magic to dull it.

I'm able to do so much more than when I first fought Lord Loss's familiars. It's frightening. I'm not in control of myself, just reacting, doing things without knowing how. The magic part of me isn't even giving me instructions now. It's bypassing the conscious part of my brain, working by itself.

More of the cast and crew stumble through the hole. Several of the demons in pursuit try to tear through after them. I scatter the monsters, then quickly establish a second barrier around the hole, which allows humans through but not demons.

A heavy thudding sound. Dervish and Lord Loss have crashed to earth. Still struggling with each other, both wounded and bruised, roaring spells and curses.

The familiars make a coordinated attack, ganging up on me. They close from all angles, encircling me. I try backing up to the wall of the barrier, to guard myself from sneak attacks, but a few have already gotten in behind me. Artery — neck fixed and hot for revenge — snickers. I sense the confidence of the demons. They have me trapped. My situation should be hopeless. But the magic part of me only sees this as a way to deal with them all at the same time.

I find myself rising into the air, then turning, slowly at first, then at great speed, three-hundred-and-sixty-degree spins, around and around, creating a vortex. The demons are sucked towards me, collide, and are thrown clear. I'm not

injured by the collisions — my skin has automatically tough-
ened.

A couple of demons try to fight the bite of the wind and
drag me down, but all are repelled. Eventually they quit and
return to harassing and killing other humans. I drift back to
the ground. Slightly dizzy but otherwise fine, I do what I can
to protect the fleeing crowd, trying to shepherd through as
many as I can.

There aren't many coming now. The stream has died away
to a trickle. No sign of Bo returning. I wonder how long we
have left, if she'll have time to make it back. As if in answer,
Dervish bellows, "We have to get out! It's going to close!"

"You'll never leave!" Lord Loss screams, digging a couple
of hands deep into Dervish's flesh. The snakes in the demon
master's chest are spitting at Dervish's face, trying to bite him.

"Go!" Dervish shouts. "Save yourself!"

"As if!" I snort, eyeing up Lord Loss. I focus on his lumpy,
writhing arms. With a cruel smile, I gnash my teeth together — and all eight of his limbs are abruptly severed.
Stunned, he topples backwards, yelping with pain and shock,
his disconnected limbs flopping to the ground.

Dervish crumples up into a weary ball. I hurry to my uncle, grab him, and toss him through the hole in the barrier as
if he was a frisbee, using magic to soften his fall. A quick
glance at Lord Loss. I can't resist the opportunity to toss a final movie-style quip his way. "Some people say you're a
badass — but I think you're pretty 'armless!" Then I skip out
before he recovers and rips me to pieces.

BITTERSWEET

✠ ✠ ✠

I feel the difference as soon as I step through the hole. Magic drains away from me instantly. Tiredness sets in. My left arm and shoulder ache like no pain I've experienced before. But I'm not completely powerless, not yet. I face the gap in the barrier, summon the final dregs of my magic, and prepare myself to fight any demon that tries to follow us through.

Dervish groans and forces himself up, helped by a trembling Bill-E. One of Lord Loss's hands is embedded in the flesh of his stomach. He pries it out and tosses it away. It twitches for a few seconds, then disintegrates into an ashlike substance.

I see humans running towards the barrier. "Faster!" I scream. "You don't have much longer! You've got to . . ."

Lord Loss glides across the face of the hole, blocking my view. His face is a mask of hatred and fury. Snarling, he starts to come through . . . then pauses, looks around, and drifts backwards.

"He doesn't dare cross," Dervish mutters. "His magic would fail him out here. He'd have to fight on our terms."

"You will suffer for this," the demon master snarls. "Your deaths would have been horrible, but now they'll be far worse now. I will find new ways to —"

"Yeah, yeah," Bill-E says, stepping up beside us. "Go blow it out your rear, you pathetic waste of space."

Lord Loss hisses and starts to spit out a spell. Before he completes it, there's a sharp cracking sound and the hole in the barrier seals itself. Lord Loss looks up and down, in case there's any crack remaining, but it's been completely repaired.

"I will answer your insults later," he vows, new arms forming from all eight stumps. He looks at his new arms and smiles witheringly. "You will die at these hands eventually. Only now it will be much slower and far more excrutiating than I had originally planned."

Glancing backwards, the demon master flexes his fresh fingers and points at the people still fleeing Slawter, those trapped within the bubble of magic.

"For now, watch as I content myself with this sorry bunch." Having delivered his threat in a manner any movie demon would be proud of, the eight-armed heartless monster floats towards the doomed humans, warding off his familiars, saving these last few victims for his own warped pleasure.

"Look away," Dervish says wearily to those of us on the safe side of the barrier. "This is going to be ugly. You don't want to watch."

"We have to get them out!" a woman wails. "My son's still in there. You have to go . . ."

Dervish looks at her darkly. Puts a finger to his lips. She

falls silent. Then my uncle turns his back on the town, sits on the ground, and very slowly and deliberately closes his eyes and places both hands over his ears — blocking out the sights and sounds of the inhuman, bloody slaughter.

✠ Dervish is right. It's not something that should be seen. Yet I have to watch, at least for a while, as Lord Loss savages and slaughters one person after another, dragging them kicking and screaming up close to the barrier, so we can see and hear more clearly. It's dreadful, the ways he finds to torture and kill them. I want to reach through and stop him, but my powers are swiftly fading. Even if there was some way of breaking though the barrier, I no longer have the strength to harm him. I'd have to go back in, but that would be suicide.

Juni regains consciousness while Lord Loss is hard at work. Groans, sits up, looks around groggily, then leaps to her feet, eyes wide. "It's OK," I tell her. "We made it. They can't —"

"What happened?" she shouts, striding up to the barrier, stopping just short of it, studying the bloody scenes within, astonished, on the verge of tears.

"You were knocked out," Bill-E tells her. "We pulled you through."

"But . . . the barrier . . ." She touches it. Pulls her hand back quickly when she feels the power.

"The hole's gone," I explain. "It was only temporary. We got out as many as we could. The rest . . ." I shake my head sadly.

Juni stares at Lord Loss and his victims, her pale skin flushed, dried blood caking the back of her head where she was struck. She's trembling with confusion and fear, like the rest of us. I think about giving her a hug but I'm too tired. So I just stand and stare with her.

Gradually we all turn away from the horrific scenes, sickened, weeping and shaking, grasping each other for support and comfort. I'm one of the last to look away, watching for Bo, hoping against hope that she'll show, that another hole in the barrier can be opened, that I'll be able to get her out.

But she doesn't appear. She's either still looking for Tump and Abe or — more likely — has been killed by a demon. If the latter, I hope it was quick and painless, though I don't suppose it was. Who'd have thought that of all the deaths today, Bo Kooniart's would hit me hardest.

Eventually I look around and do a quick head count. Thirty-four. Of all those working on the film . . . hundreds of people . . . only thirty-four remain.

I'm about to sit, when one of the faces catches my attention. Slowly, incredulously, I march across and glare with contempt and hatred at a bruised, dazed, but very much alive Chuda Sool.

"*You!*" I snarl. He looks up timidly. "How dare you? So many dead because of your treachery, but you sit here among the living, meek as an innocent child. You should have stayed behind with your masters!"

"Please," Chuda croaks. "I didn't know . . . they said . . . I thought . . ."

"You knew!" I scream. "They said they'd spare you — that's the only thing you got wrong. That's your only complaint." I grab his head and force him to look at the destruction on the other side of the barrier. "You made this happen! They're dying — dead — because of *you!*"

Chuda starts to cry — but with fear, not regret. "Don't hurt me. Please . . . I can help you . . . I know spells. They promised me a long life, hundreds, maybe thousands of years. How could I say no? Davida convinced me. She set this up. She's the one you should blame."

"Davida's dead," I growl. "She got her comeuppance. Now you will too."

I reach deep within myself for the dwindling flames of magic, intent on destroying this traitor.

"No, Grubbs," Bill-E says quietly, laying a hand on my right arm.

"He deserves it!" I yell.

"He probably deserves a whole lot worse," Bill-E agrees. "But it's not for you or me to pass judgment. We don't have the right to take his life. You'll become a killer, no better than any of those demons, if you murder him."

"It's execution, not murder," I growl.

"Different word, same thing," Bill-E says. "It's wrong. You'd hate yourself."

"He's right," Juni says, leaving the barrier and stepping up on my other side. "You're a child, Grubbs. No child should ever kill." Chuda smiles at her pitifully, but her eyes are hard. "Especially when there are plenty of capable adults around," Juni whispers, then grabs Chuda's head with both hands. His eyes fly wide open — then fill with a white light. He gibbers madly, trying to knock her hands away, but Juni holds firm, pumping magic into Chuda's brain, frying the circuits, her mouth twisted into a wicked leer.

Chuda falls back when she releases him, jerks a few times, then dies, face contorted, skin black at the sides of his head.

Bill-E and I gape at Juni, shocked. Dervish is staring at her too, along with most of the people around us.

"I did what I had to," Juni mutters, looking away to hide her shame. "He had it coming. We couldn't let him walk away, not after . . ." She gestures at Slawter.

"B-b-b-but . . ." Bill-E stutters.

"Don't," Juni stops him. "The last thing I want right now is a child lecturing me about ethics." She walks off, rubbing her hands up and down her arms.

"Leave her," Dervish says sadly. He looks over his shoulder and spots Lord Loss finishing off another of his playthings. Sighs and stands. "Let's gather everybody together and get out of here. I've had enough of demons."

How do you explain away a massive demonic killing spree? Easy — by covering it up and pretending it was an accident.

Dervish spends the rest of the evening making calls, to the Disciples, police, politicians, journalists, firemen, doctors, and nurses. The Disciples have a network of contacts, ready and waiting to smooth over the cracks when something like this happens. It's how they've managed to keep previous crossings quiet in the past. They come in droves, the first arriving late at night, setting up camp close to the barrier around Slawter, so they can move in swiftly and mop up when the time is right.

They keep the survivors together for four days, in vans and tents brought to the site by more of Dervish's contacts. Nobody's allowed to leave or make a call. Counselors work hard, making the most of the time, trying to help people stave off nightmares and come to terms with the deaths of relatives and friends.

Waiting for the demons to finish off the last few victims and return to their own universe. I often feel like going back to the barrier, to view the devastation, to curse Lord Loss or just stand there and let him curse me. But I don't.

The barrier finally dissolves when the last of the Demonata take their leave. Dervish and a team of volunteers enter the town and demolish the magical lodestone in the D warehouse, closing the tunnel between universes. When the threat of a follow-up invasion has been averted, they retrieve the bodies (and body parts), stack them in buildings around the town, then set the place on fire. It's a gruesome end for the unfortunate victims, but necessary to mask the demonic marks and trick the outside world into believing they died in a ferocious fire.

That's the official story, built on the bones of Bill-E's gas leak rumor — there was a massive explosion and a wave of fire swept through the town with brutal speed, killing most of the cast and crew. I doubt if all the survivors will stick to it. I'm sure a few will protest in the months and years to come, tell their friends, go to the media, try to spread the truth. But who'll believe them? If anyone goes on a TV show, prattling on about demons, the audience will think they're a maniac.

The teams destroy the film reels too. Davida's notes. The models, props, costumes. A thorough job, leaving nothing behind, removing all traces of the Demonata, planting fake evidence in its place. The only people who knew what the film was about were all in Slawter. As far as the rest of the world will ever know, Davida Haym's last movie was going to be a departure from her earlier movies — a love story with a touch of science-fiction.

I think, if Davida is watching in some phantom form, that will hurt the most. Not the deaths, the betrayal by the demons, her own grisly slaughter. But that her film was destroyed and all traces of her masterpiece removed.

Good! I hope her ghost chokes on it.

✠ Standing beside Dervish as the fires rage, the night sky red and yellow, thick with smoke. Watching Slawter disappear forever. Most of the survivors and emergency crew are with us. Silence reigns.

"It's over," Dervish says as the roof of a large building — maybe the D warehouse — caves in with a raucous crash, sending splinters of flames flickering high up into the sky. "In the morning we can leave. Everyone can go."

The sweetest words I've ever heard.

✠ Juni is gone before we awaken. She leaves a note for Dervish. She's been quiet and withdrawn these past few days, not saying much, refusing to discuss the mayhem or her killing of Chuda Sool.

In the note she says she's confused. She knows Chuda was guilty, deserving of punishment, but she can't believe she acted so callously. Her whole world has changed. She knows about demons now, and she's seen a side of herself that she doesn't like. She needs time alone, to reflect, consider, explore. She says she has strong feelings for Dervish, but doesn't know if she ever wants to see him again. Tells him not to look for her. Promises to visit him in Carcery Vale one day — *if*. That's the last word — *if*. I think she meant to write more, but couldn't.

Dervish doesn't say anything when he reads the note. Just hands it to me and Bill-E once he's done, then goes for a long, lonely walk. I'd help him if I could, say something to make him feel better. But I don't know what to say. Bill-E doesn't either. So we don't say anything when he returns, only stay close in case he needs us.

✠ The evacuation proceeds smoothly, people leaving without a fuss, driven home or to train stations, airports, wherever. Some of the counselors travel with the worst affected, not only to comfort them, but to make sure they don't harm themselves or wind up in trouble.

I think some of the survivors won't be able to live with what they've witnessed. This will haunt all of us, but it will hit some harder than others. I think there will be a few more deaths in the years to come.

I'd like to do something to help the worst afflicted, but I can't. It's not possible to save everybody. Even heroes have their all-too-human limits.

✠ By four in the afternoon the last cars are leaving. The media has been told of the supposed fire, and news teams begin to arrive, eager to scour the ashes of Slawter — renamed Haymsville for the benefit of the rest of the world. They're angry to find none of the survivors here, and they hit the roof when they learn that the emergency crews were on the scene so long before them. But there's nothing they can do about it except moan.

I watch with little interest as the reporters circle the skeletal remains of the town. I've had enough of the place. I just want to forget about it. Put it behind me and move on.

Bill-E is beside me, silent as a corpse. He's kept himself busy in the aftermath, spending a lot of time with the other children who made it out alive, talking about what happened, trying to help. That's been his way of dealing with the tragedy. He doesn't want time alone to think about it, to remember, to fear. At night he wakes screaming, but in the day he fights the memories. What will he do when we're home and he has nothing but ordinary life to occupy his time? What will *I* do?

"They didn't find all the bodies," Bill-E says. "I heard Dervish talking about it with another Disciple. The demons took some people back to their universe. Maybe Bo was one of them. Maybe she'll escape and return. I'm sure it's possible. I mean, Dervish did it, right?"

I grunt negatively in reply, knowing in my heart that Dervish would have told us if there was even the slightest glimmer of hope.

I turn to face Bill-E. I instinctively know that this is the right moment, the one I've been waiting so many months for. Time to tell him that we're brothers.

"Bill-E . . ." I begin, but before I get any further, Dervish appears.

"Hey," he says with forced good humor. "You want to stay here all night or are you coming with me?"

"Coming where?" Bill-E asks, turning, and the moment is lost. I won't make the great revelation, not now. Later. When another good time comes around.

"Yes — where?" I ask, turning like Bill-E, so we're both looking at our uncle.

"Where else?" Dervish says with a thin, weary smile. "Home."

A LITTLE CHAT

✠   ✠   ✠

I T'S strange, trying to settle back into everyday life, not telling anyone about Slawter, acting like normal people who've merely survived a very human tragedy. Bill-E and I lie to our friends, make up stories about the filming, describe the fire and how we were lucky to escape. Not a word about demons.

Bill-E stays with us the first few nights, despite the objections of Ma and Pa Spleen. Nightmares galore, both of us. Remembering. Screaming. Crying. Talking with each other and Dervish, trying to cope. Ironically, considering how this all started, Dervish sleeps like a baby. The confrontation was a tonic for him. It blew the cobwebs from his head, helped him out of the bad patch he'd been stuck in. The fighting, the cover-up, getting in touch with the other Disciples, discussing ways to keep the truth secret . . . all of that was nectar to my uncle. It fired up his engines. He was in his element dealing with the demonic fallout. I'm not saying he enjoyed it, but he needed it. That's his real work.

I wish it was so easy for me, that I could go off, find a demon, have a fight, purge myself of the bad memories and fears. But I took nothing positive out of what happened in Slawter. I'm just disgusted, tired, and afraid. I'm sure it will be years before I can sleep properly. If ever.

But the show must go on. The charade has to be maintained. So Bill-E returns to Ma and Pa Spleen. We go back to school. We force ourselves to focus on homework, friends, sports, TV, music, day-to-day life. We pretend that's all there is to the world, that there's nothing more frightening in life than a surprise test or saying something stupid in front of your friends and having them laugh at you.

And sometimes — just sometimes — I almost believe it, and for a little while I forget about Lord Loss, Davida Haym, Bo Kooniart, Emmit the demons, the dead. And life is the way it should be, like it is for most people. But the sensation never lasts. It can't. Because I know the truth. I've seen behind the curtain of reality. I know that monsters *are* hiding underneath a billion beds across the world. And I know that sometimes . . . more often than we imagine . . . they come out.

✠ "Time for that talk."

We've been home for nearly three weeks after our return. I'm in the TV room, some comedy show playing on the big screen, not really concentrating. When Dervish sits beside me and speaks, I'm not sure what he's talking about. Then, as he switches off the TV, I remember. In the middle of the madness he said that if we got out alive, we'd have to have a chat about my magical prowess.

"You were amazing in Slawter," Dervish says. "Magic was pumping through you and you had complete control over it."

"I just tapped into the power in the air," I shrug uneasily. "No biggie."

Dervish smiles. "Modesty's becoming, but let's not bull ourselves — you were on fire. You did things I can't even comprehend. When I was fighting Lord Loss, I noticed some of the demons trying to get through the hole in the barrier. You kept them back. How?"

"I established a second barrier around the hole. Demons couldn't get through it but humans could."

Dervish chuckles. "Do you realize how difficult that is? I couldn't do it. Even when I was in Lord Loss's realm, at my most powerful, I couldn't have pulled off something like that. I don't know many who could."

"It wasn't like I planned it," I say, for some reason feeling edgier the more he praises me. "I reacted to what was going on around me. The magic told me what to do. I wasn't in control. I couldn't do any of it again. I don't even remember most of what I did."

Dervish studies me closely, his expression serious. I sense his reluctance to continue — and with a jolt, I guess the reason why, and instantly understand why I've been so nervous.

"The Disciples are few in number," Dervish says quietly. "We're always on the lookout for new recruits, but most mages never realize their magical potential. It lies dormant unless they have an encounter with the Demonata. Even then there's no guarantee that it will develop, that we'll be able to make use of them."

"No," I say softly.

Dervish frowns. "I haven't asked you anything."

"I know what's coming. And the answer's no. Please don't ask me." I look away, trembling, fighting hard not to cry. "I hate it, Dervish — the demons, the battles, the madness. I don't want to face Lord Loss or anything like him again. I don't want to become a Disciple."

A lengthy silence. Finally Dervish sighs. "I'd spare you if I could. But there are so few of us and we're so limited. From what I saw in Slawter, you could be one of the most powerful Disciples ever. You might even . . ." He clears his throat. "You might even be a true magician. Like Bartholomew Garadex."

"No way!" I cry. "You told me I wasn't. You said magicians are born that way, that their powers are obvious from birth."

"I know. But the way you handled yourself . . . Maybe I was wrong. Maybe there are late-developing magicians. But even if you're not a magician," he says quickly as I start to protest, "you *are* part of the world of magic. No normal person could have done what you did. You have a very powerful, important talent, and it would be a crime to deny it. I know you don't want to involve yourself with the Disciples, but you have to. Some of us believe that the universe creates champions, that a few humans in each generation are given the gift of magic in order to protect this world from the Demonata. If you've been chosen by the universe . . ." He smiles shakily. "You can't say no to a calling like that, can you?"

"Just watch me," I snap.

Dervish's expression darkens. "You're acting like a child."

"Well, duh! Haven't you noticed? I *am* a child! Big for my age, but don't let size fool you. Try me again when I'm old enough to vote."

"I can't wait that long," Dervish says. "Magic must be nurtured. Every day we hesitate is a day wasted. When you face your next demon, you might —"

"There won't be a next!" I shout. "Weren't you listening? I don't want to join your band of do-gooding Disciples! I said *NO!*"

"Unacceptable," Dervish replies flatly. "You have a responsibility. I know it's hard — I've gone through it myself — but you have to be who you are."

"You don't know anything!" I hiss. "You didn't lose your family to demons. You didn't have to fight Lord Loss when you were my age. You haven't felt the terror of . . . of . . ." I'm breathing hard, hands clenched, tears in my eyes.

"You can't let fear rule your life," Dervish says. "Everyone's afraid when they face a demon. We learn to mask our fear, but it's always there, chewing away at us. Fear . . . doubt . . . wishes that we weren't magical, that we didn't have this cross to bear. I can help you overcome that fear. I can show you the way."

I stare at him heavily. There's no point arguing. He really doesn't understand. I'm not just afraid — I'm horrified. In Slawter I did what I had to. It was an unreal situation and I had no choice but to let the magic wash through me and use it to fight my way out. But I hated the whole experience and I have no desire to repeat it. I'm through with the universe of demons. I've done more than my fair share. Gotten the better of them — and saved lives — twice. That's enough.

I start to tell Dervish this, to try to make him see it from my point of view. But all that comes out is a sigh, then a sullen, "Anyway, it's irrelevant. I'm not a magician or a mage. It was just a Slawter thing."

"You're wrong. The power is there. We have to develop it. You can't —"

"What if it isn't?" I interrupt. "What if I'm just an ordinary kid who did something weird and wild, but is back to normal now? Would you leave me alone then?"

He frowns. "Yes, of course. If the talent isn't there, obviously we can't fan it into life. But it is. It must be."

"Look for it," I challenge him. "Can you find out if a person has magic in them or not?"

Dervish nods. "We can't in people who haven't tapped into it, but once someone unleashes their power, it's always there. I can search for it, find it, prove it to you. I should have done it before, after you fought Vein and Artery, but I wasn't thinking straight when I returned from my battle with Lord Loss."

"Go on then." I face him directly. "You won't find anything, but if you want to look, feel free."

Dervish puts his hands on my shoulders. My left arm's still sore from when it was cut off. I wince, but steel myself and grunt for him to continue. I'm not sure why I'm so confident that he won't find anything. But I am.

Dervish's eyes close. "Relax," he says. "You'll feel a force . . . an intrusion. Try not to fight it. I'll get out as quickly as possible."

I let my eyelids flutter shut. Seconds later I sense a presence, a soft probing, like fingers creeping through the corridors of my brain. I tense against it.

"Relax," Dervish murmurs. "It's OK. I won't hurt you. Trust me."

It's hard, but I do as Dervish says, opening myself up to him, letting him probe deep . . . deeper. I feel him closing in on a part of myself that I wasn't aware of a few months ago. I know that if he finds it, he'll continue pestering me to become a Disciple. He won't give up. He'll keep on and on, and eventually I'll cave in and let him train me. And that will mean facing the Demonata again. More pain, craziness, terror.

Something moves within me. A pulse. A shiver. Hard to define. Like when you think you catch a movement out of the corner of your eye, but you're not sure, and when you look closely, nothing's there.

My eyes open. Dervish's forehead is creased, his lips moving. I close my eyes again. Smile faintly and let him continue. Warm now, safe, at ease.

Finally Dervish releases me. When I look at him, he's shaking his head, confused. "I don't understand. I was certain. You shouldn't have been able to . . . if there was nothing there . . . if you're not a mage . . . It doesn't make sense!"

"I assume that means no magic," I grin.

"Not even a trace. I thought I was zooming in on it, but then . . . nothing. I kept on looking, went deeper than necessary, because I was so sure . . ."

"You can try again if you want," I tell him.

"No point." He manages a brief smile. "It's either there or it isn't. I'd have found it if it was. You can't hide magic, not from those who know what to look for. I was wrong. You were right. You're clean."

"So I don't have to sign up? The Disciples can struggle on without me?"

Dervish pulls a face. "I don't know. The magic isn't there now, but I suspect, if we placed you in an area of magic again, or took you into the universe of the Demonata. . . . Our leader, Beranabus, is more powerful than any of us. He spends a lot of time among demons. Perhaps . . ."

I feel fear creeping back, but then Dervish scowls. "No. I'm not going to sign away your life to him. Maybe you'll choose to go down that path when you're older. But I don't have the right to pass that sort of a sentence on you. Beranabus plays rougher than the rest of us. I've seen how he treats those closest to him, and I wouldn't wish it on anyone."

"Then I'm free?" I say hopefully. "I don't have to . . . ?"

"No." Dervish smiles, warmly this time, pleased for me, even though he's disappointed not to have found a powerful new recruit. "Congratulations, Grubbs. You're ordinary. I hope you enjoy a long, happy, boring life."

"Coolio," I laugh. Then the pair of us settle back, turn the TV on, and spend a few hours surfing channels, chatting about things deliciously unimportant.

✠ In my room. Dark. I haven't turned the light on. Sitting on the end of my bed. Thinking about what happened earlier, Dervish's probe, what it would have meant if he'd found magic, how awful my life might have been. I should be celebrating the fact that I'm not one of the magical breed. Rejoicing. But I can't. Because I know that's a crock.

I rise, walk into the bathroom, and stand in front of the sink, facing the mirror above it, even though I can't see it in the darkness. I don't want to do this. But I have to be sure.

I think I outfoxed Dervish. I think there *is* magic inside me, but it responded to my wishes and hid itself, or deflected my uncle's probe. He said that wasn't possible, but if you're powerful enough, maybe it is. I could be wrong — I'm praying that I am — but I'm not sure. And I have to be. Even if nobody else ever knows, I need to.

I focus on the lightbulb overhead. For a long second nothing happens. The darkness holds. I begin to hope.

Then the light comes on. A warm, steady, unnatural light. And the hope dies away as quickly as it was born.

I look at my scared reflection in the mirror. Make it disappear, so only the wall behind me is reflected in the glass. Then I let my reflection reappear and the light fade. I stumble back to bed. Lie down on top of the covers. Silent. Shaking. Terrified. Unable to sleep. Certain now — I'm not normal. I tricked Dervish, but I'm part of the world of magic. I can't escape. The universe of the Demonata will call to the magic within me and suck me back in. I know it will. This isn't over, not by a long shot.

There are no happy endings.

The horrifying adventures continue in

BEC

Book 4 in THE DEMONATA series

available now

from Little, Brown and Company

A BOY'S SCREAMS pierce the silence of the night, and the village explodes into life. Warriors are already racing towards him by the time I whirl from my watching point near the gate. Torches are flung into the darkness. I see Ninian, a year younger than me, new to the watch . . . a two-headed demon, pieced together from the bones and flesh of the dead . . . *blood*.

Goll is first on the scene. An old-style warrior, he fights naked, with only a small leather shield, a short sword and axe. He hacks at the demon with his axe and buries it deep in one of the monster's heads. The demon screeches but doesn't release Ninian. It lashes out at Goll with a fleshless arm and knocks him back, then buries the teeth of its uninjured head in Ninian's throat. The screams stop with a sickening choking sound.

Conn and three other warriors swarm past Goll and attack the demon. It swings Ninian at them like a sword and batters two of them down. Conn and another keep their feet. Conn jabs one of the monster's eyes out with his spear. The demon squeals like a banshee. The other warrior — Ena — slides in close, grabs the beast's head and twists, snapping its neck.

If you break a human's neck, that person will almost surely

die. But demons are made of sturdier stuff. Broken necks just annoy most of them.

With one hand, the demon grabs the head that Goll shattered with his axe. Rips it off and clubs Ena with it. She doesn't let go. Snaps the neck again, in the opposite direction. It comes loose and she drops it. She pulls a knife from a scabbard strapped to her back and drives it into the rotting bones of the skull. Making a hole, she wrenches the sides apart with her hands, digs in and pulls out a fistful of brains. Grabs a torch and sets fire to the grey goo.

The demon howls and grabs blindly for the burning brains. Conn snatches the other head from its hand. He throws it to the ground and mashes it to a pulp with his axe. The demon shudders, then slumps.

"*More!*" comes a call from near the gate. It's late — later than they usually attack. Most of the warriors on the main watch had retired for the night, replaced by children like me. Our eyes and ears are normally sharp. But this close to dawn, most of us were sleepy and sluggish. We've been caught off-guard. The demons have snuck up. They have the advantage.

Bodies spill out of huts. Hands grab spears, swords, axes, knives. Men and women race to the rampart. Most are naked, even those who normally fight in clothes — no time to get dressed.

Demons pound on the gate and scale the banks of earth outside, tearing at the sharpened wooden poles of the fence, clambering over. The one at the rear might have been a diversion, sent to distract us. Or else it just had a terrible sense of direction, as many corpse-demons do.

Warriors mount ladders or haul themselves up onto the rampart. They lock arms with the demons. Hard to tell how many there are. Definitely five or six. And at least two are real demons — the Fomorii.